A Kiss for Captain Hardy

by the same author

Novels

A SWORD FOR MR FITTON
MR FITTON'S COMMISSION
ADMIRAL OF ENGLAND
THE BALTIC CONVOY

For children

JONES'S PRIVATE NAVY

A Kiss for Captain Hardy

SHOWELL STYLES

FABER AND FABER
London   Boston

*First published in 1979
by Faber and Faber Limited
3 Queen Square London WC1
Printed in Great Britain
by The Bowering Press
Plymouth and London
All rights reserved*

© *1979 by Showell Styles*

British Library Cataloguing in Publication Data

Styles, Showell
A kiss for Captain Hardy.
I. Title
823'.9'1F   PR6037.T96K/

ISBN 0-571-11380-X

AUTHOR'S NOTE

All the chief characters in this story actually existed. All the main events actually happened.

The letters and dispatches printed in italic are on historical record and where dialogue was recorded it has been adhered to.

ONE

1

Mr Hardy came out to stand in the wooden porch of the Lamb Inn and at once the porch looked too small for its purpose. He was so broad a man that his great height was not obtrusive except by comparison with structures made for lesser men. From Spithead, invisible beyond the crooked chimney-pots of the High Street, a sou'-westerly rain-squall ceased in a splatter of wind-blown drops and the leakage from a broken spout whipped across Mr Hardy's face. It was a face large and round, weather-browned and stolid, topped by thick reddish-brown curls which extended into sidewhiskers above the cheekbones. It showed no flicker of annoyance as he passed the back of his hand across it to wipe the water from his chin.

"By'r leave, sir." An ostler lugging a heavy tarpaulin bag squeezed past the folds of his faded boat-cloak. "I see the barrow ain't come, sir—I told the lad ten sharp, sir," he added, glancing up apprehensively as he set the bag down.

The big man nodded indifferently. Having gauged the distance between the top of his head and the porch roof, he produced from under his cloak a black cocked hat and settled it firmly in place. He felt, vaguely, something symbolical in the action. Last night Tom Hardy of Portisham in Dorset had arrived at the Lamb; this morning Lieutenant Thomas Masterman Hardy of His Majesty's frigate *Minerve* was leaving it to join his ship.

"You needn't wait," he told the ostler in a deep voice that suited his bulk.

The ostler coughed and lingered insinuatingly. With visible reluctance Mr Hardy's hand groped through the opening of his cloak and produced a silver coin from the pocket of his white breeches.

"Thankee, sir."

The ostler retired into the inn grinning wryly. A shilling, as he'd expected; Mr Hardy had stayed overnight at the Lamb before. Any other officer of a King's ship would have made it half-a-guinea—but Mr Hardy was an odd fish anyway. Any other officer would have damned and blasted fit to burst when he found the barrow wasn't waiting.

Mr Hardy's quick ear had detected the rattle of the barrow before it came round the corner with a ragged boy pushing it. The boy halted his barrow, knuckled his forehead, and tried to lift the tarpaulin bag. Mr Hardy took it from him one-handed and heaved it effortlessly onto the barrow.

"Sally Port," he said briefly. "Stay on the quay till I come."

The tarpaulin bag was trundled rapidly away, its owner stalking after it at a more dignified rate. The blustery morning, more like April than October, had followed the heavy shower with a burst of sunshine that set the wet Portsmouth cobbles gleaming like gold. He flung open his cloak, revealing the blue coat with white cuffs and lapels, and tilted his head back to sniff the salt-laden air, thus displaying the one remarkable feature of his face—a chin that jutted like the beakhead of a first-rate. The rain-squall had almost emptied the High Street and the few people who were beginning to emerge from houses and shop-doorways were townsfolk hurrying on their interrupted business. For once there was not a drunken seaman in view, nor any uniformed man except himself. Here as in Portisham, reflected Mr Hardy, it was difficult to believe that England was approaching the crux of a struggle for her very existence.

His shore leave had been a very short one. The circumstance that *Minerve* had been sent home with dispatches from the squadron off Genoa had given him the chance of seeing England for the first time in three years, and of spending a week at the old house in Portisham with his parents, two brothers, and six sisters. *Minerve* would sail for the Mediterranean again tomorrow and her second lieutenant was glad of it. Twelve of his twenty-seven years had been spent at sea and his real home was on board a ship; but there was a stronger reason for his eagerness to sail. He knew that a sea confrontation with the enemy must be imminent. This new French general, Bonaparte, had with victory after victory taken most of the north Mediterranean seaboard for his country. The Spaniards, allies of the French, were not likely to tolerate the presence of a British fleet in those waters for much longer, seeing that they had three ships of the line for every two in Admiral Jervis's scattered squadrons. There would be a great battle soon—perhaps the decisive battle of the war—and Mr Hardy wanted to be present when it took place.

There were small things as well as great to be attended to, however. He needed a new pair of razors. He was crossing the street to Harrington's the cutler's when a shrill cry came to his ears from the direction of the inn.

"Mr Hardy! Tom!"

Mr Hardy halted and turned. A chaise had stopped in front of the inn and an elderly lady in a grey dress was descending from it with the aid of the postillion. Nearer at hand a girl in a white gown and a cherry-coloured mantle was running towards him across the cobbles, clutching a large and floppy bonnet to her flying black ringlets with one hand. Mr Hardy was displeased. He had made his farewells with Susan Manfield at Elworth three nights ago; she was part of the curiously unreal Portisham life he had closed the door on when he donned his cocked hat. His annoyance showed only in a slight compression of his lips, and he doffed the hat with a correct flourish as she approached. After all, it was understood in Portisham that he and Susan would be married when she came of age. Her brother John, the family lawyer of the Hardys, was affianced to Tom Hardy's sister Catherine and everyone —including Tom Hardy—agreed that the match with Susan was a very suitable one.

"Tom!" Susan, stumbling to a halt, dropped a perfunctory curtsey. "Aren't you surprised to see me—and pleased, too?"

"Of course," growled Mr Hardy.

"You don't—look it, sir," she panted. "But then—you never do." She took a deep breath. "Aunt Deborah's with me and we stayed the night with Mr Dervill at Hambledon and drove down early specially to see you off and the man at the inn said you'd gone and I *am* glad you hadn't. Do you like my new bonnet?"

There was perhaps a faint twinkle of amusement in Mr Hardy's deepset blue eyes, but if so it was transient. He inspected the bonnet cursorily.

"Well enough. Not suited to Portsmouth on a squally day, Miss Manfield."

Susan pouted. She was eight years his junior and extremely pretty; a craft, in Mr Hardy's opinion, as trim as anything in her class. She had come a long way to see him and his rigid sense of justice told him that he was not returning a fair reward. Much as he disliked contrived speeches, deeming them dishonest, he felt moved to attempt one for Susan's benefit.

"It's a pretty bonnet," he went on, awkwardly enough. "But not so pretty as you are, Susan."

Unaware that he was ruining his effect, he took his watch from his fob and glanced at it as he was speaking. Susan, between laughter and tears, made the best of it.

"That's a *little* better, Tom. Now you must come and bid goodbye to Aunt Deborah—and we'll take a glass to your safe voyage."

A glance told him that Aunt Deborah had gone into the

Lamb, and another at the low black cloud hurrying over from the south-west showed her wisdom.

"I've no time at all for your aunt and very little for you," he said bluntly. "My dunnage is waiting on the quay and I'm due on board—"

"Oh, we know you're never late and always keep appointments," she began petulantly, and checked herself, her brown eyes softening. "You must go, of course. But Tom—you *did* only kiss my hand at Elworth. Won't you—?"

She tilted her head back and closed her eyes, red lips pursed invitingly. The threatened squall broke in that instant, wind and rain striking with the suddenness of a blow. The new bonnet flew off and went scuttling over the cobbles with Mr Hardy in close and surprisingly agile pursuit. He overtook it in three long strides, crammed it anyhow on the girl's head, and spun her round with her back to the storm. White rods of rain were driving aslant to ricochet in six-inch fountains. He pulled the hood of the cherry-coloured mantle over her head and administered a gentle push.

"Run for it," he commanded gruffly.

Susan ran two steps and turned. "Oh, Tom—"

But Mr Hardy was already a large vague shape retreating through the silver curtains of the rain.

The squall had almost blown over when he came down to the quay but a thin rain still drifted across the grey-green water. The ragged boy scrambled out from beneath his barrow and was told to wheel it to the edge of the quay. Hardy hailed a two-oar wherry from among the craft clustered farther along the quay; *Minerve* was lying a mile inshore from Gilkicker Point and the distance was not worth the hire of a lugger. He gave the ragged boy his tuppence as the wherry came tossing alongside and lowered the tarpaulin bag into the bows himself —it contained among other things two fresh Abbotsbury hams and a brace of the streaked double-Dorset cheeses—before stepping down into the sternsheets and grasping the tiller.

"Frigate *Minerve*," he growled.

The bow oarsman shoved off and the wherry headed out from the quay, slamming into the chop of the waves.

Susan Manfield had lingered in Hardy's thoughts for perhaps thirty seconds after he had left her but she was quite forgotten now that there was salt water under him again. He was his proper self once more, a sea-officer expert in his profession and dedicated to it. To excel in it was his ambition, and if he though of the possibility of promotion it was with a philosophical realisation of its remoteness. Promotion to post-captain, nine times out of ten, came of influence in high places, and he had none whatever; the tenth chance was of a bloody ship-to-ship battle ending in victory and promotions all round, a chance that most lieutenants would never meet with. He was in any case content as second lieutenant of *Minerve*; though (he admitted it to himself) it would be satisfying to board her from a captain's gig with a smart crew instead of from a half-rotten wherry stinking of fish.

The wherry was pounding into the larger waves of Spithead now. A dim grey shape loomed like a detached cliff through the rain-haze to larboard—the old *Agamemnon*, in for a long-overdue refit. Beyond her lay a lesser shape at sight of which he gave an involuntary gulp, swallowing rare emotion. That was *Minerve*. Forty guns, 18-pounders on the maindeck, French-built and the fastest frigate in the service, she had been taken by the *Lowestoft*, 32, off Genoa sixteen months ago. Her present captain George Cockburn—Dandy George to the lowerdeck—and her first lieutenant, Culverhouse, were amiable enough as men but in Hardy's opinion too lenient with their ship's company; it was Hardy's stern interpretation of their edicts that was largely responsible for her efficiency as a fighting ship, his unvarying practice of strict justice untempered by mercy that had welded her 300 men and boys into a united crew aware of its strength. As her long hull and three tall masts grew out of the grey obscurity the big man at the wherry's tiller felt the pride of a craftsman in his work and the only real affection he had ever experienced.

The high wooden side with its row of black gunports rose overhead. A sharp hail from the deck was answered by the stroke oarsman with the "Aye-aye!" that indicated the arrival of an officer. Hardy stood up as the tossing boat sheered alongside and handed the man his two shillings. A line came snaking down in answer to his peremptory shout and the tarpaulin bag was drawn up. Waiting for the lift of the wherry's stern he sprang neatly to the dangling ladder, and it was in that moment that he remembered the new razors he had intended to buy. The unexpected meeting with Susan Manfield was responsible for the lapse; but both were small matters compared with this homecoming to *Minerve*.

Ashore in the coffee-room of the Lamb, Susan Manfield snuffled tearfully between sips of hot coffee while Aunt Deborah, perplexed but sympathetic, eyed her with concern.

"But, dear, he's a most honest and upright young man," said Aunt Deborah. "I'm sure he means well by you—"

"I know all th-that." Susan clattered her cup impatiently. "It's no use if he doesn't love me, is it?"

"My dear! It's plain enough that his heart is yours, surely."

"His heart?" muttered Susan. "Aunt, I don't believe he has one."

"Drink your coffee, dear," said Aunt Deborah, shocked.

Susan obeyed. A tear ran down her nose into the coffee. She drank that too.

2

From where he stood on *Minerve*'s quarterdeck a pace behind Lieutenant Culverhouse Hardy could look beyond the black pot-hats of a double rank of marines to where the Rock's dark cone, half-a-mile away across the ruffled water, soared into low clouds. Between the mass of shipping in Gibraltar harbour and the polished wood of the quarterdeck rail he could see Captain Cockburn's gig pulling fast towards the frigate. He shot a keen glance round him to assure himself that all was ready, though he knew quite well that it was; not every day did a Commodore hoist his broad pendant on board this ship. The side-boys in white gloves, three on either side of the entry-port; the two bosun's mates with their silver calls slung round their necks; Lieutenant McIntyre of the marines within nudging distance of his drummer and two fifemen; Gage and Maling, third and fourth lieutenants, in their proper places—like himself they were dressed in their best uniforms; a midshipman and a seaman at the main signal halyards; for'ard on the larboard side the gunner and the five gun-crews who would fire the salute. All correct. Another two minutes and the gig would be alongside.

"Never met the Commodore, Hardy, have you?" said Culverhouse over his shoulder.

"No," said Hardy.

"An odd fish. Up in the air one minute, down in the dumps the next. Likes to talk—but don't cross his hawse, because he's never wrong. Serve out the soft soap. He likes—ah!"

The gig appeared for a moment framed in the opening of the entry-port and vanished below the frigate's side.

"Stand by, all!" snapped Culverhouse.

A brief order, a rattle of oars, and then a large cocked hat with gold lace on the brim rose into view. Beneath it was a smallish man pale and meagre of face, whose blue coat and white breeches hung like a scarecrow's apparel on a body thin to the point of emaciation. Captain Cockburn's round ruddy face and plump figure, appearing behind him, made an emphatic contrast. As the Commodore stepped onto the quarterdeck with a hand to his hat something approaching pandemonium broke loose. The marines' drum, McIntyre's roar of "Pre-*sent*!", the piercing squeal of the bosuns' pipes, and a discordant shrilling of *Heart of Oak* from the fifes, all burst out simultaneously. The Commodore walked slowly forward with his hand still at the salute, very erect and preternaturally solemn, with Cockburn close behind him. They halted in front of Culverhouse just as the uproar ceased.

"My first lieutenant, sir—Mr Culverhouse," Cockburn said.

The Commodore dropped his hand and extended it for Culverhouse to shake.

"We renew acquaintance, Mr Culverhouse," he said in a high tenor voice. "You attended one of my dinner-parties on board *Agamemnon*."

"And Mr Hardy, sir, second lieutenant," Cockburn proceeded.

Hardy, shaking the claw-like hand, found himself looking down at an angular face that was little short of ugly—long thin nose with deep grooves drawn from nostril to lips, one eye bright and the other dull under a drooping eyelid. Then the Commodore smiled and there was a curious change, for the smile had a singular sweetness which (thought Hardy) had something womanish about it.

"A pleasure, Mr Hardy. I shall hope—"

Bang! The first gun of the salute interrupted the Commodore in mid-sentence. From the corner of his eye Hardy noted that the broad pendant had been hoisted and broken-out at the right moment.

"—to have further conversation with you," the Commodore went on. "Though I see," he added, looking up at the lieutenant's towering height and waiting until the second gun had exploded, "that it may be a tall order."

Cockburn laughed, in Hardy's opinion a good deal more loudly than the jest merited, and Commodore Nelson passed on to be introduced to the remainder of *Minerve*'s commissioned officers while the eleven-gun salute thundered to its end. Like an echo of the guns came the roar of cannon from the frigate *Blanche*, at anchor two cable-lengths to starboard; she was to sail in company with *Minerve*. Her cable, Hardy noted, was up-and-down like that of his own ship. Culverhouse had warned him that there was to be no delay in making sail, and the one thing he found to approve of in the Commodore was the speed with which Nelson got through the ceremony of introductions. Cockburn's shout came sooner than he had expected.

"Mr Culverhouse! We'll get under way at once. Make the signal to *Blanche*, if you please."

Hard on the heels of Culverhouse's snapped orders came Hardy's enormous voice, exploding like another gun as he ran to his station for'ard, sending the fo'csle men to the capstan and the topmen racing aloft to cast off the gaskets. The deck emptied itself of idlers as if they had been swept away with a broom. *Minerve*'s sails filled, her yards were braced round, and she gathered way on the larboard tack with *Blanche* heading to take up her station three cable-lengths on the starboard quarter. The Rock under its cloud-cap diminished slowly astern. Close-hauled, the two frigates began their thousand-mile voyage eastward.

Commodore Nelson had shifted his flag from the *Captain*, 74, to the much faster *Minerve* because of the urgency of his mission. Nelson was carrying orders from Admiral Jervis for the complete evacuation of the isle of Elba by the British— garrison troops, civilians, and Sir Gilbert Elliot with his staff. Sir Gilbert had been Viceroy of Corsica until the Cabinet in London had ordered the evacuation of Corsica and the withdrawal of the British Fleet from the Mediterranean. So much Hardy knew from what the first lieutenant had passed on to him of Captain Cockburn's information. Of the wider implications he knew little and cared less, it being his belief that a sea-officer wasted his time in giving thought to anything other than his ship and his duty. He was to have enlightenment thrust upon him from an unexpected quarter.

The Mediterranean was in no friendly mood that December. The easterly levanter persisted, blowing half-a-gale at times, and shaping a course for Elba was a slow business. For *Minerve*'s watch-on-deck the contrary wind meant hard and ceaseless toil, sheets and braces to be handed every time she went about, royals furled or shaken out as the wind allowed; the smaller *Blanche* had great difficulty in keeping station in the thick weather and high seas. Cockburn needed landfalls with which to check his dead-reckoning and the Spanish coast was never more than a mile or two over the horizon to larboard —since the summer of 1796 that coast of friendly harbours had become an enemy coast. The main Spanish fleet was known to be at Cadiz but there were certainly frigates and possibly larger fighting-ships at Cartagena and Alicante, Valencia and Barcelona, so that the frigates were to run the gauntlet of attack for a good 700 sea-miles. Culverhouse had masthead lookouts at their stations day and night, for there was a moon behind the low clouds and therefore the possibility of sighting an enemy vessel in good time. Hardy made it his business to see that every man on the lower decks was aware that the pipe to quarters might sound at any moment.

For the first three days of the voyage the second lieutenant saw nothing of the Commodore, and his first unfavourable impression of Horatio Nelson was not improved by Culverhouse's report that he was suffering from severe seasickness and could not leave his cabin. He had evidently recovered on the fourth day, for such officers as were not on duty were bidden to dinner at three o'clock with the Commodore in the captain's day-cabin, an invitation which Hardy, who had the afternoon watch, was unable (with relief, for he detested dinner-parties) to accept. From remarks that Culverhouse let fall he gathered that it was not a cheerful occasion, the Commodore being in low spirits— "miserable as a whore in a nunnery" were Culverhouse's words —on account of the slow progress they were making. Slow indeed it was. They had sailed from Gibraltar on December

14th and by the night of the 19th had got no farther than a position some ten miles south of Cartagena, having taken five days to cover 300 miles. Towards midnight of the 19th, however, the wind veered a point to southward, allowing the frigates to end their long bout of tacking and thrash along close-hauled with the steady breeze broad on the starboard bow.

Hardy had the morning watch on the 20th. In theory two commissioned officers kept a watch together, and on this morning watch Hardy's presumptive partner was the captain; but Cockburn was not a man to spend four hours walking the deck at night when he had a reliable officer to do it, and was accustomed to put in one or perhaps two brief appearances during a watch. On this occasion Hardy came on deck a few minutes before eight bells of the middle watch. At four in the morning it was still a long time to dawn, but the low clouds that sped above the leaning pyramids of dark canvas were luminous with diffused moonlight. A yellower and more concentrated light came from the poop lantern, which was kept alight as a guidance for *Blanche*. Culverhouse's lean shape came to the helm to meet him and his saturnine features were suddenly revealed by the binnacle lamp in front of the helmsman.

"Course nor'-east by east, Mr Hardy," he said. "This wind's holding steady. You'll have an easy watch."

"Maybe," said Hardy, who was no believer in prescience.

"Masthead lookout was relieved at six bells. Welling's aloft now."

Welling was an old Fleet seaman and knew his duty. It was at Hardy's suggestion that the night lookouts were being selected from men who could be trusted to stay alert. Culverhouse called the fourth lieutenant from his station for'ard and went below. Hardy checked the course, eyed the straining canvas critically, and began his walk up and down the windward side of the quarterdeck. *Minerve* was lying over at a moderate heel but her deck was steadier than it had been for three days. The medley of sounds that came to his ears was a very familiar one: the high unvarying chord of the wind in the rigging, the hiss of the black waves alongside, the low-voiced murmur of the men of the deck-watch just reaching him from where they squatted along the rail beside the guns. He had made the journey from after-rail to mizen mast and back three times when he was aware of a slight figure mounting the slant of the deck towards him. The Commodore's high-pitched voice hailed him.

"Is that you, Mr Hardy?"

"Yes, sir."

Hardy halted his pacing and put a hand to his hat as Nelson joined him. He was not pleased at the prospect of having to converse with an officer so many steps of rank above him.

"I'm an ill sleeper of late," the Commodore said. "You'll allow me a part in your watch, I hope."

"Of course, sir." The more politic "It will be a pleasure, sir" was not within the scope of Hardy's honesty.

"Then pray continue your walk."

The two men began their pacing to and fro. Nelson had pulled up the hood of the cloak he was wearing to secure his hat against the wind and in the faint light resembled a skinny old woman. Hardy had a vision of the comical sight they must present, himself a foot taller than his companion and twice as broad, and was glad of the obscurity that partly hid them from the eyes of the helmsman and the midshipman of the watch farther for'ard. They took two turns in silence before the Commodore spoke again.

"I take it Captain Cockburn has made you aware of my mission, Mr Hardy," he said abruptly.

"He has, sir."

"And what is your opinion of it?"

Hardy was taken aback. It crossed his mind that it was unusual, even derogatory of naval discipline, for a Commodore to ask the opinion of a second lieutenant upon any matter whatsoever. However, a reply was required of him.

"I've no doubt it's—um—necessary, sir," he said.

"Necessary?" Nelson turned the end of the word into a kind of screech. "It's no more necessary than—than striking all *Minerve*'s topmasts to lessen this confounded heel." His slip on the wet and tilted planking a few seconds earlier provoked the adjective. "And far more dangerous, Mr Hardy. Dangerous to the conduct of this war. We need every ally we can get to help us beat the French, and over there to northward are Naples, Sicily, Genoa—" He checked himself a trifle breathlessly. "Mr Hardy, if you could bring yourself to shorten your stride I'd be obliged."

"Beg pardon, sir." Hardy reduced his long paces by a half.

"They look north and they see the French army conquering all before them. They look south—and they see the British Fleet running away. They're too weak to do other than choose the winning side. What will they do, think you?"

"Put it like that," Hardy began slowly, "I'd say—"

"They'll open their arms to the French," Nelson swept on unheeding, "and the fault will be ours. Not yours or mine, Hardy, nor the Admiral's, but the fault of those timeservers in London who—"

He stopped himself quickly. They were turning at the after-rail, and in the dim radiance of the poop lantern Hardy caught a glimpse of his companion's thin face twisted as if in agony. Taking it too much to heart, this little Commodore. Had to get it out to someone, no doubt, and criticism of Cabinet policy in front of a post-captain like Cockburn wouldn't do. He was right, though. Running away did no good, least of all to British ships and men.

"We could have kept Corsica by action, fighting action," Nelson was saying, less excitedly now. "We could keep Elba. Instead we abandon both and let ourselves be kicked out of the Mediterranean. Doubtless their Lordships have in mind that the French and Spanish and Dutch fleets outnumber ours by two to one. But don't they realise, Hardy, that one British seaman is worth three of theirs? Don't they know that every man in every ship is ready to lay down his life for his ship, his King, and his country?"

Hardy doubted that last statement very much. The crews of jailbirds and pressed landsmen and drunken ruffians flogged and bullied into seamen had few idealists among them. He felt, however—with a rare impulse of sympathy—that it would be cruel to say so to this odd little man.

"You may be sure, sir, that whatever happens every man aboard *Minerve* will do his duty," he said.

The Commodore, turning in mid-stride, slipped again on the spray-wet deck and Hardy shot out a hand to grip his arm and steady him. Through the cloak he felt what seemed a fleshless bone.

"Duty?" Nelson cried impassionedly. "Of course we shall all of us do our duty—if our masters will but let us. I conceive it my duty to obey orders and therefore I go to Elba. But England's duty is to save Europe from the French, and to do that she must strike with her Navy. Consider, Hardy—"

Up and down, up and down they paced, while *Minerve*'s second lieutenant was initiated into his Commodore's idea of strategy; a strategy far beyond the ship-manoeuvring which was Hardy's interpretation of the word. Holland, now the Batavian Republic, would try to take control of the south-eastern waters but the Channel Fleet must and would defeat them. The grand aim of the British should be to keep absolute command of the seas off the French and Spanish coasts. What mattered France's conquests on land if all her ports were closed to trade and all her ships rendered helpless? The fleets of France and Spain were the obstacles to this command, therefore they must be attacked and destroyed immediately they appeared at sea.

"And never was a battle more necessary than it is now,

Hardy." Nelson thumped fist into palm as he walked. "A great victory could redeem us even now, despite this craven running-away. You and I know we can beat the Dons, and Spain will challenge us first. If the Admiral—"

His voice ceased suddenly and both men halted, Nelson laying a hand on his companion's arm. The hail from the masthead came again.

"De-e-eck there! Light on th' stabb'd bow!"

Hardy cupped his hands and roared against the wind. "How far distant?"

Welling's reply came after a pause. "Could be two mile, sir. Closin' us."

"That's not *Blanche*," Nelson snapped.

"No. She'd not be that far off station. Most likely—"

"Deck!" The look-out's shout was urgent. "I can just make 'em out, sir—there's two sail, frigates."

The Commodore swung round and struck his palms smartly together. "Spaniards out of Cartagena. Mr Hardy, we'll clear for action."

His words were a command, but for a moment Hardy hesitated. That was an order *Minerve*'s captain should give. Nelson seemed to understand his hesitation.

"Clear for action!" he repeated sharply. "I'll inform Captain Cockburn myself."

He was gone, scuttling down the quarterdeck ladder at a very undignified speed. Hardy bounded to the taffrail and sent his great voice for'ard and down into the waist in a string of orders. With hardly a pause the frigate woke into noise and seething movement. Before the squeal of the bosuns' pipes had ceased the marines' drum was rattling out its furious tattoo. A medley of yelled commands accompanied the uprush of men from below, some racing to man the for'ard and quarterdeck 12-pounders while others surged like a dark flood along the maindeck beneath to separate into orderly crews at the twenty-four 18-pounders.

"All guns load!" bellowed Hardy. "Starboard gun-captains, double-shot your guns!"

The enemy frigate—if she was an enemy—had not time enough to cross *Minerve*'s bows, and since she would not willingly abandon her weather-gauge she was practically certain to attack from starboard. That first double-shotted broadside needed no request to Captain Cockburn for permission. The loud calls of the gun-captains reporting their readiness were beginning when he turned to find Captain Cockburn on the quarterdeck with the Commodore at his elbow. Nelson had thrown off his cloak and was slapping his hat impatiently against his ill-fitting breeches. Culverhouse came hurrying aft and saluted.

"Ship cleared for action, sir," he said, addressing captain and commodore impartially.

"Very well, Mr Culverhouse." Cockburn stepped to the weather rail and peered into the luminous night. "What's the latest news of these frigates?"

"With your leave, sir," Hardy said, "I'll take a look myself."

He swung himself into the mainshrouds without waiting for Cockburn's assent and hauled himself swiftly upward. For a man of his bulk he was surprisingly deft and agile and he was proud of it; he found, to his astonishment and displeasure, that he was hoping that the Commodore was watching him. Just below Welling's eyrie at the foot of the main topgallant mast he stopped, clinging to the narrowing shrouds, the whistle of the wind and the creak and groan of the yards in his ears.

"Closin' fast, sir!" Welling called down. "Spanishers for sure, they are."

He could see them plain enough, scarcely a mile away now. From this height the crinkled sea was pallid with reflection from the moonlit clouds, and the two approaching frigates, one ahead of the other and under all plain sail, were fast-moving black shapes on the water. Glancing astern, he saw *Blanche* half-a-mile away and almost in line with *Minerve*; signals were useless in this light but she must have seen the frigates by now. He returned his gaze to them, noting that both were large for their class—at least as large as *Minerve*. Their converging course with a beam wind made it a matter of only a few minutes before they came within effective range. He was about to descend when he saw the second of the two dark silhouettes change its shape, altering course as though to pass astern of *Minerve*.

Hardy climbed rapidly down the shrouds and made his report to the captain. "It's my opinion, sir," he added, "that the second frigate's heading to tackle *Blanche*."

"So we're pairing off, are we?" Cockburn drawled. "Well, I pity the fair *señorita* that falls to our lot. Carry on, Mr Hardy—and of course you'll wait my word to fire."

"Aye, aye, sir."

Hardy turned to the quarterdeck ladder. As with most frigates of her class, *Minerve*'s quarterdeck extended from the poop to the mainmast and her foredeck from the foremast to the bows, passage between the two being made possible by the gangways on either side above the open waist of the maindeck below. Battle lanterns had been slung from the deckheads below the gangways so that the guncrews underneath could see to load and fire, but the dim light from the clouded moon overhead seeped into the waist and revealed the men grouped at the 18-pounders and the hurrying small figures of the boys bringing up powder and shot. Hardy, who had charge of the maindeck guns in action, glanced keenly round the deck and then took a position halfway up the ladder whence he could keep an eye on the quarterdeck as well as on his guns. From here he could see nothing of the sea or the enemy frigates, but the voices of captain and commodore came to his ears above the background of gruff orders and metallic clicks from the marines, who were ranked on the poop loading their muskets.

"She comes on well, whoever she is," Nelson commented, his high voice trembling slightly.

"She does, sir." Cockburn sounded a trifle perturbed. "If she intended a collision she couldn't come on better. She's well within range now—I've a mind to open the ball."

"No. We only assume she's a Spaniard, captain. We must be certain."

In the pause that followed Hardy heard clearly the hiss of wind in canvas and the rush of waves along a ship's side, faint at first but swiftly growing louder. His ear told him that the strange frigate had closed to within thirty fathoms distance.

"Running board-and-board, by God!" said Cockburn. "If we don't fire first—"

"Wait!" rapped Nelson.

Hardy saw him fling his hat to the deck and spring onto the weather rail with one hand clutching the mizen shrouds. His long hair streaming in the wind looked as white as his breeches in the dim light. You damned little fool, thought Hardy, if there's a loaded musket ready for you—

"Aho-oy!" The Commodore's shrill voice pierced the noises of wind and waves. "This is a British frigate. If you don't bear away I shall fire into you."

The reply came at once, and—surprisingly—in English, deep and measured tones ringing down the wind.

"This is the Spanish frigate *Sabina*, and you may fire when you damned well please!"

Cockburn waited no longer. Hardy's enormous bellow echoed his order an instant later as the lieutenant sprang down to the maindeck.

"Fire!"

Sabina's broadside was simultaneous with *Minerve*'s in a deafening thunderclap.

3

Minerve's running fight with *Sabina* lasted for more than two hours. For most of that time Lieutenant Hardy strode slowly up and down the miniature Hades of the maindeck, a superintending demon amid a host of furiously-toiling lesser demons. A more imaginative man would have been struck by the resemblance of his surroundings to the popular conception of the Pit—the hellish din, the flashes of red fire, the black mephitic smoke, the writhing half-naked figures dimly perceived. The faint light from the night sky overhead was quickly banished by the dense clouds of powder-smoke whirling upwards, for the guns were firing into the wind and the smoke blew back through the ports with a transient irradiation from the long jet of crimson flame at each discharge. But noise was the overwhelming impression. After that first stunning detonation of a twelve-gun broadside fired in unison the 18-pounders exploded at irregular intervals, their ear-splitting blasts interspersed with the banging of the *Sabina*'s guns and the frequent splintering crashes, as of a wooden door smashed with a sledge-hammer, when the enemy balls struck between rail and waterline. *Minerve* was built of Adriatic oak and her hull was stronger than the hulls of most British-built frigates, but the twelve open gun ports in her starboard side were necessarily large and through them, from time to time, came death.

Hardy was experienced in single-ship actions; in *Hebe* and and *Meleager* he had learned the value of his calm presence and his steady stride to the men at the guns. An 18-pounder required ten men to handle it efficiently. There were one hundred and twenty men hauling and striving at the guns of *Minerve*'s maindeck and he could put a name to any powder-blackened face momentarily lit by a gun-flash; a sharp word here, a crude jest there—when the uproar allowed it—and the fever-heat of their spirits was maintained. At the end of the first hour two of the hundred and twenty were dead and nine wounded, their places being taken by men from the skeleton crews standing by the larboard guns. Most of the wounded had been gashed or transfixed by splinters struck from the frames of the gunports and sent flying like javelins through the smoky gloom, but one of *Sabina*'s 18-pounder balls had hurtled clean through a port and taken the heads off a gun-captain and one of his crew. Hardy's pacing had to be done with care lest he should slip in the unseen pools of blood.

It took a well-trained crew two minutes to reload. There were thus brief lulls in the loudest of the noise and in them Hardy could hear the banging of the upper-deck 12-pounders and the flat reports from the marines' muskets. He found himself hoping that the Commodore had sense enough to keep well down the lee side of the quarterdeck where a Spanish musket couldn't take aim at him. Once a sharp crack and a thrashing of canvas, followed by a chorus of shouts, told him that one of *Minerve*'s spars had been shot away, the driver yard probably, and a few minutes later one of the great blocks from the mainmast rigging crashed down into the maindeck a yard behind him as he strode. His ear was cocked for orders from the quarterdeck but in that first hour none came. This was unlike those other sea duels, all of them in daylight, when there had been manoeuvring for position and respite for the guns. *Sabina* was simply holding her weather-gauge without shortening sail and pounding away at her enemy's starboard side.

A respite came at last. A yell from one of the gun-captains that he had no mark to fire at was followed instantly by a roar of cheering and then by Cockburn's screech from the quarterdeck.

"Mr Hardy! Cease fire!"

The Spanish frigate's foretopmast was down. *Minerve* shortened sail to keep board-and-board with her and there was a short interval during which the gun-crews, having sponged out and reloaded, could relax in loud excited chatter.

"Quiet, there!" rasped Hardy; and so was able to hear his captain's order to resume firing.

Again the deafening racket began. Hardy, whose imperturbability was a shield deliberately forged after his first sea-fight, wondered dully how long his eardrums would be able to stand it. A fearful metallic clang and a high-pitched shrieking hurried his steps aft to where one of the 18-pounders, struck full in the muzzle by a ball from *Sabina*, had been flung backwards off its carriage, crushing three men beneath it. Two of them were dead, smashed to red pulp. The third, still alive and squealing like a pig, was pinned to the deck under the dismounted gun; the massive breech-end had crushed his lower body across the loins. In a few minutes he would be dead. Meanwhile he was in agony. The 18-pounder weighed nearly two tons.

"Put him out," Hardy shouted above the thunder of gunfire.

The man he addressed, who was holding the heavy rammer, hesitated. Hardy seized the rammer from him and swung it sideways against the dying man's head. The screaming stopped.

"Lash the breeching to the pomelion!" Hardy yelled at the half-stunned gun-captain. "Lively, now—I don't want this gun running wild on the maindeck!"

His perception of that imminent danger helped him to close his mind to what had just happened. He realised suddenly that he had been able to see the danger because the smoke-filled maindeck had become lighter, and when he bent to peer out through the gun-port he saw why. Daybreak had come. There was *Sabina* across the intervening space of heaving dark-grey waves, only one or two of her guns still firing—a mockery of the fine frigate she must have been two hours ago. Foremast and mizen were mere stumps with untidy cordage flying from them and her main topgallant mast hung by its tangled stays with the torn sail flapping. As he looked, he saw the main topmast bend and fall with all its hamper, and heard them cheering on the upper deck above him. The maindeck gunners echoed the cheer.

"Stand to, there! She's not struck!" he roared.

But before the guns had fired another half-dozen rounds

Cockburn's order to cease firing reached him above the noise of another cheer, loud and prolonged this time. *Sabina* had struck her colours.

Hardy mopped his brow and looked round him. It was light enough to see the gun-crews, some collapsed exhausted beside their guns, other grinning and shaking hands, all with their naked torsos black from the powder-smoke and glistening with sweat; light enough to see the litter of splintered wood and the wet dark stains on the deck. In two places the Spanish shot had holed her planking and through the larger hole he could see the bows of *Minerve*'s longboat, evidently just lowered. He called a leading seaman and ordered the wounded at the dismounted gun to be carried down to the cockpit, stepped out of the way of the carpenter's party who had arrived to examine the damage, and was making for the ladder when Captain Cockburn's voice came down to him.

"Mr Hardy! Come on deck, if you please."

The upper deck showed every sign of the fierce and prolonged action. *Minerve* had been brought to the wind and was lying-to, all her masts standing but the sails in tatters and the rigging blowing out astern. Half the weather rail had gone, the deck was splintered and grooved by the shot, and there were a score of wounded men, some of them in the red and white of the marines, lying about waiting to be carried below. With a curious relief Hardy saw the Commodore, hatless and smiling, standing at the broken rail looking towards the defeated Spaniard.

"Mr Hardy," Cockburn said, "I'm sending Mr Culverhouse and yourself to take over *Sabina*. You can't get sail on her as she is, so I'll pass a tow. You'll have six men as prize crew —I can't spare more." He turned to the first lieutenant, whose left arm was sleeveless and crudely bandaged. "Captain and officers will be sent to *Minerve* in the longboat as soon as you've boarded her, Mr Culverhouse."

"Aye aye, sir."

31

"And when you've secured her crew do nothing more—hail me the moment the tow's well bitted. We've run too close in to Cartagena and I want to be under way with the least possible delay."

Hardy climbed down into the waiting longboat and gave Culverhouse a hand as he followed. The boat shoved off and they pulled across a wallowing sea that was already reflecting the pale yellow of approaching sunrise beneath the grey clouds. As the boat rose on a crest Hardy caught a glimpse of two vessels lying hove-to about a mile to the westward.

"Blanche?" he queried.

"And her prize," nodded Culverhouse, nursing his arm. "Must have had an easier task than we did, judging by their top-hamper. All masts standing, as you see. *Minerve*'s mainmast is cut half through, by the bye, and won't stand t'gallant and royal. It'll be a slow passage to Elba."

Hardy reflected that the frigate could no longer hope to escape if she was chased by a superior force; but as usual he kept his thoughts to himself.

"There's the cutter putting off with the line," Culverhouse said. "Pull, you lubbers, pull—they'll have the tow rigged before we board at this rate!—Wonder what her butcher's bill is," he added, staring at *Sabina*, now a pistol-shot away. "Ours ain't too bad, I fancy. Ince and Smith the gunner were killed —poor Smith was cut in two by a ball, clean as whistle—and thirty-odd wounded. How was it on the maindeck?"

"Five killed. Maybe a dozen wounded."

"H'm. It'll look well enough in a Gazette.—My Christ, look at that!"

The longboat was drawing close to *Sabina*'s battered flank. From the scuppers below what was left of the rail blood was still draining in long streaks and tendrils. There was no time for further comment because they were alongside. Culverhouse hauled himself awkwardly up to her deck, the watchful Hardy following and ready to check any slip. They were confronted by the Spanish captain. He was a tall man of haughty mien, and his swarthy face sent an irrelevant flash of memory across Hardy's mind: a visit he had paid to Hampton Court some years ago. Culverhouse, who was proud of his Spanish, began to address him in that language and was summarily cut short.

"I am Don Jacobo Stuart, captain of this vessel," said the Spaniard loftily in English. "I surrender her only because I have lost sixty of my men including all my officers. My sword I shall give up to no one but your captain."

"The boat will take you to *Minerve*, sir," said Culverhouse. "Permit me to say that you fought most gallantly. And to felicitate you on your excellent English. Your name—"

"I am the great-grandson of James Stuart, king of England, Scotland, and Ireland," interrupted the captain brusquely, and climbed wearily down into the longboat.

Hardy nodded to himself; he had seen a portrait of James the Second in the Hampton Court gallery and the likeness was remarkable. An odd trick of fate but there was no time to think about it. The cutter bringing the line across from *Minerve* was passing the longboat as she headed back to the frigate, Cockburn could be heard shouting urgently, and *Sabina*'s upper deck was a cross between a shambles and a dockyard rubbish-heap. Dead and wounded men lay everywhere, on or under the piles of broken spars and cordage and tattered canvas. Tired bloodstained ragamuffins that had once been smart Spanish seamen were lugging their living messmates out of the chaos and carrying them below. Culverhouse sent Hardy for'ard with three of the armed seamen who had boarded *Sabina* with them while with the other three he set about getting what was left of her crew below decks. The line was brought aboard and as the hauling of the 13-inch cable to which it was attached began Hardy tailed-on with the rest. At last the dripping rope was brought to the bitts and made fast. As Hardy turned from signalling the fact to the watchers on *Minerve*'s quarterdeck Tomlin, one of the seamen, spoke.

"*Blanche* is under way with her prize, sir. Makin' signals, too."

The two vessels were close-hauled, fast closing *Minerve* who was herself wearing what sail she could set on her wounded masts and beginning to move through the water. Hardy could make nothing of the flags that streamed from *Blanche*'s yardarm and concentrated on the business in hand. Culverhouse shouted from aft that he had a man at the helm, and half-a-minute later the first jerk came on the tow-rope. *Sabina* lurched, recovered, and started to gather way. Three knots, thought Hardy, watching the straining tow; that's all we'll make with this wind. *Blanche* and her Spanish prize had already overtaken *Minerve* and were flying on ahead. As if their passing had caused it, there was renewed activity on Cockburn's ship and all hands appeared to be on deck.

"Sail on th' labb'd quarter!"

Culverhouse had sent one of his men to swarm up the stump of the mainmast and the hail came from him. Hardy remembered Cockburn's comment on their nearness to Cartagena.

"Two sail there is, sir—frigates, I reckon."

There was to be a chase, then—and it wouldn't last long. Stand and fight? *Minerve* could still put up a fight, but Culverhouse and himself with half-a-dozen seamen could do nothing to help her. And the Commodore had an important mission to Elba.

"Deck! Two more sail, astern of t'others. Line-o'-battle ships."

Minerve's second lieutenant showed his rare perturbation by taking his right ear between finger and thumb and tugging at it. Then he hurried aft, jumping over torn bodies and clambering through the wreckage of the main topmast. Culverhouse, looking worried, was standing by the helmsman.

"Mr Culverhouse," said Hardy formally, "I submit that we should cast off the tow."

"Cast off?" The first lieutenant gaped at him. "Without orders?"

"You're in command here," Hardy said stolidly. "It's plain *Minerve* can't run for it as we are, and run for it she must."

Culverhouse bit his lip and scowled. "Captain Cockburn will cast-off himself if he needs to."

"D'you think the Commodore would let him? That man's a sentimental fool. He'd forfeit a frigate and his mission rather than abandon us, Culverhouse." Hardy, unwontedly emphatic, rammed his point home as the other hesitated. "We'll be taken in any case. Why give 'em *Minerve* too?"

Culverhouse glanced astern. The Spanish frigates were hull-up from the deck now and fast approaching under all sail.

"Very well, but—"

Hardy was twenty yards away already. Picking up a boarding-axe that lay among the wreckage he ran to the bitts and with two mighty blows severed the taut cable. He saw *Minerve* yaw and recover as the strain left her stern, but she held her course. He turned his attention to the pursuing ships. On they came, the bow-wave under their stems visible as they sped towards *Sabina*, two of the smaller class of frigates mounting twenty-eight guns. They could catch *Minerve* and hold her in play until those line-of-battle ships came up—unless *Sabina* could somehow delay them. It occurred to him suddenly that to the approaching frigates *Sabina* must look like an abandoned hulk, not worth their attention.

When Tom Hardy had to translate thought into action he could do so with a celerity very different from his usual deliberate methods. Less than five minutes later the leading frigate, espying a British flag flying from the mainmast-stump with the Spanish colours beneath it, altered course and signalled her consort to do the same. It may have been with relief that her captain abandoned the chase of a powerful British frigate in order to recapture the prize so impudently flaunted under his nose, and a futile banging of pistols as his boat approached *Sabina* helped to ease his conscience. The British flag was hauled down, however, as the boat came alongside, and the two British officers on board surrendered their swords to the Spanish officer who confronted them. One of the two was a big man with a grimy face; beneath the grime was something very like a grin.

4

"Christmas Day in the workhouse," said Lieutenant Culverhouse, massaging the hand of his wounded arm. "I don't suppose the Dons'll give us turkey and mince-pie."

Lieutenant Hardy grunted. The two men were sitting in wooden chairs on either side of a bare table on the morning of December 25th. The room, in a wing of the barracks adjoining the Captain-General's mansion at Cartagena, had walls of whitewashed stone with a small barred window high up on one side and an oaken door, locked and bolted, in the opposite wall. A truckle-bed stood at each end. Through the window, which afforded a view of a blank wall opposite, came the jangle of church bells. It was very cold.

This was their sixth day of imprisonment. As *Minerve*'s captain had surmised, the course of the frigates during the running fight had brought them close in to the mainland, and within four hours of their capture Hardy and Culverhouse were being marched under escort from the quay of Cartagena harbour to be interviewed by the Captain-General of the Department of Cartagena. His Excellency Don Miguel Gaston, a tubby little man with a disproportionate grandiloquence, had treated them kindly enough and had been genuinely distressed by their refusal to give their paroles; a refusal, as he pointed out, which would deprive him of the pleasure of entertaining them at his own table. The dismal room they now inhabited was the alternative, with exercise twice a day in the barrack yard under the eyes of a couple of slovenly Spanish soldiers.

But they had been neither starved nor neglected. A surgeon who announced himself as Don Miguel's own doctor had come in to dress Culverhouse's wound, pronouncing it in a fair way to heal, and the meals were adequate though too highly flavoured for Hardy's taste. If they had hoped for a chance of escaping, however, they were disappointed. Cartagena was the main naval arsenal of Spain and the barracks where they were imprisoned housed the numerous troops guarding the arsenal; a pair of lambs in Smithfield Market were as likely to get clear away, said Culverhouse gloomily. And it might be months, even years, before they were exchanged.

To his own surprise Hardy did not share this view. *Minerve* had still been in sight when the Spanish frigates had recaptured *Sabina*; likely enough the Commodore had been watching through his glass. He had no high opinion of Nelson's prudence, or for that matter of his common sense, but he had an odd conviction that the little man would not forget them.

"Come on," Culverhouse said, getting up. "Clear the deck and let's walk."

By pushing table and chairs aside and running the truckle-beds into the corners they could obtain nine paces along the length of the room. Hardy did this and they began their walking up and down, hands behind backs, turning inwards towards each other at the end of each short march. Half-a-dozen turns, so Culverhouse said the first time they tried it, made their prison feel homelike despite its unstirring deck of stone flags.

They walked for some minutes in silence. Unprecedentedly, Hardy broke it.

"What d'you make of the Commodore?" he asked abruptly.

"Make? Of Nelson?" Culverhouse sounded surprised. "I never sailed with him, you know. Talked to officers who have. He seems to be like ginger—it's fiery, and you either like it or you don't. I told you when he came aboard that he thinks he can do everything and he's never wrong, or won't accept that he's wrong."

"He doesn't believe in looking after himself."

"He don't run away from enemy shot, if that's what you mean. Dixon of the *Agamemnon* told me he's all the time hunting two foxes, glory and promotion."

Hardy considered this for two turns. "I suppose we're all hunting those," he said at length.

"Well, Nelson's got a head start of us," said Culverhouse. "Post-captain at twenty, he was. That's what comes of being nephew to the Comptroller of the Navy. He must be thirty-seven or thirty-eight now and he'll be a rear-admiral before he's forty."

"Married?"

"Aye. Colonial widow a bit older than himself." Culverhouse frowned sideways at his fellow-prisoner. "What's come over you, Tom? Damned if I've ever known you take so much interest in anyone, unless it was that madman at Chatham who swore he could make an iron ship to float."

A faint trace of embarrassment showed itself on Hardy's large countenance. "I dunno," he mumbled. "It's just that he strikes me as being like a child. Wants someone to look after him."

"You'd better apply for the post," said Culverhouse derisively. "Nursemaid to the Rear-Admiral—"

His mockery was cut short by the sudden opening of the door. The squat sergeant who was their jailer entered with two soldiers armed with muskets behind him and addressed a brief sentence to Culverhouse, whose Spanish was adequate for comprehension.

"We're haled before the Captain-General," he said to Hardy. "Maybe we're going to get a Christmas dinner after all."

A lengthy march along echoing passages ended in a splendid room all mirrors and tapestries where the portly Don Miguel sat at a huge table covered with stamped leather. The Captain-General, excessively genial, smiled and nodded at the two who stood before him and spoke at some length to Culverhouse.

The first lieutenant's lean face showed surprise, then pleasure, and finally puzzlement. He turned to Hardy when Don Miguel had finished his speech.

"Seems we're to embark at once for Gibraltar, Tom," he said. "It's an exchange, far as I can make out. Though how that can be, when we've only been here—"

"*Sirvase leer esto?*" interrupted Don Miguel, beaming.

He handed a paper to Culverhouse and Hardy looked over the first lieutenant's shoulder to read it.

"*Sir,*

The fortune of war put La Sabina into my possession after she had been most gallantly defended; the fickle Dame returned her to you with some of my officers and men in her.

I have endeavoured to make the captivity of Don Jacobo Stuart, her brave Commander, as light as possible; and I trust to the generosity of your Nation for its being reciprocal for the British officers and men.

I consent, Sir, that Don Jacobo may be exchanged, and at full liberty to serve his King, when Lieutenants Culverhouse and Hardy are delivered into the garrison of Gibraltar.

HORATIO NELSON
Commodore"

TWO

1

"Permit me to fill your glass, Mr Hardy," said Colonel Drinkwater. "So. Now—as I understand it from the Commodore, it was by your action on board *Sabina* that this vessel was saved from capture. How did you come to—ah—pitch upon that idea of hoisting the flags?"

"Easy enough," muttered Lieutentant Hardy, scowling at the broiled chicken he was attacking. "Any numbskull would have thought of it."

The Colonel sighed, not quite inaudibly; this great block of a lieutenant was tough material, even for a best-selling author accustomed to interviewing. He tried again.

"Suppose those Spanish frigates had fired into you. They might have done so?"

"They might." Hardy drank some wine and returned to his chicken. "But they didn't."

Colonel Drinkwater gave him up and turned to his neighbour on the other side, who was vivaciously describing to Sir Gilbert Elliot his part in the siege of Calvi. Commodore Nelson, at any rate, was always ready to talk about his doings.

The four men were at three o'clock dinner in *Minerve*'s day-cabin and *Minerve* was under way and fast leaving the Rock astern to eastward. Her two passengers, the ex-Viceroy of Corsica and Colonel John Drinkwater of the Viceroy's staff, were on their homeward way from Elba, whence at this moment the transports with the garrison were also sailing for England. Drinkwater, cultured and handsome, esteemed himself an author and with reason; his *Siege of Gibraltar*, dedicated to His Gracious Majesty, had run into three editions in three years and was still selling. Even at the dinner-table he had notebook and pencil at his elbow. The frigate had paused at Gibraltar only long enough to take on board Culverhouse and Hardy, restored to their ship after release from Cartagena and a six weeks' wait at the embattled port below the Rock, for it was known that the Spanish fleet had sailed to try and unite with the French fleet off Brest and that Admiral Jervis proposed to intercept them.

It was not only Colonel Drinkwater's perquisitions that were making Lieutenant Hardy disgruntled, despite his pleasure at being once more at sea in *Minerve*. Two hours before the time the Commodore had appointed for his "dinner-party", two sail that had been sighted astern had been identified as Spanish, a frigate and a ship of the line, and *Minerve*'s guns had been cleared away ready for action. The pursuers had gained a little on their quarry and Drinkwater had asked the Commodore whether he thought an action possible, Hardy being present on the quarterdeck at the time.

"Very possible," returned Nelson; then, with a stage gesture at the broad pendant flying at the masthead, "but before the Dons get hold of that bit of bunting I'll have a struggle with 'em. Sooner than give up this frigate, sir, by God I'll run her ashore!"

The disgusted Hardy, wondering whether this was aimed at the literary Colonel's notebook, found Nelson's bright left eye upon him and was abashed. He was bidden peremptorily to dinner with Sir Gilbert and Colonel Drinkwater, Captain Cockburn and the first lieutenant remaining on deck to watch the enemy. And here they all were making polite conversation and sipping wine as though some likely accident—a change of wind or the advent of another Spanish ship ahead of them—

might not at any moment bring *Minerve* to bay. Drake playing bowls while the Armada approached had never been a hero of Hardy's. He could hear Nelson responding to Drinkwater's questions in his high voice, voluble and self-confident.

"The loss of sight in one eye, Colonel, was a small price to pay for Calvi. What I feel more, sir—for I am a man—was the praising of others for services I alone rendered at Calvi. One hundred and ten days I was engaged against the enemy at sea or on shore. I was in three actions against ships, I commanded four boat actions, I—"

I—I—I, thought Hardy; he felt ashamed, as if it was he, not Nelson, who was speaking. And yet he could not forget the warmth of the Commodore's welcome when he had come on board with Culverhouse, the grip of the thin hand and the genuine feeling in his words—"I was never more glad of a meeting than now, Hardy." There had been no play-acting in that, for sure.

Sir Gilbert Elliot, on Nelson's right, was addressing him across the table. Hardy inclined to like Sir Gilbert, a neat middle-aged man with a pleasant Scots accent who usually spoke but little and always to the point. This afternoon, however, the ex-Viceroy—perhaps because there was a fair chance that he would be dodging cannon-balls shortly—had taken enough wine to make him loquacious.

"I fancy you didn't hear me, Mr Hardy. I was saying that Naples would make a fine Fleet base, the Gulf being so sheltered. You have been there?"

"*Minerve* watered there last summer," Hardy responded politely. "I didn't go ashore."

"I made a tour of the Italian states in the autumn," said Sir Gilbert, balancing his wineglass against the motion of the frigate, "and was most hospitably received at the Embassy. The wife of our ambassador there, Lady Hamilton, has great influence with the Queen and I am persuaded the establishment of a British base—"

Hardy listened with half-an-ear. The shouted orders on deck were sending topmen aloft to trim the set of the maintops'l.

"—a remarkable woman," the ex-Viceroy was saying; the wine seemed to have induced a confidential tendency in him. "A woman who'll stick at nothing to get what she wants. A face to haunt a man's fancy. But her figure—alas!" He lowered his voice, leaning across the table. "Nothing short of enormous, Mr Hardy. I can admire a fine woman—"

"Man overboard!"

The shrill cry from the deck was loud enough to halt all conversation in the cabin. Hardy, muttering an abrupt apology, was on his feet and out of the cabin before the other three had uttered a word. Captain Cockburn was at the poop rail gazing astern at the frigate's wake, Culverhouse was yelling at the hands who were working furiously to get the jolly-boat slung outboard. No speck could be seen on the long trail of white turbulence that stretched away eastward from *Minerve*'s rudder, but beyond it on the ruffled grey sea the sails of the two Spanish vessels lifted, the smaller of the two white triangles in advance of the larger.

"I'll go, sir," said Hardy.

"You'll have to look damned sharp about it, Hardy," said Cockburn uneasily. "I can't wait for you."

"I know that, sir."

The jolly-boat splashed down and her crew dropped into her. Hardy sprang into the sternsheets and she shoved off. As soon as the men gave way the westward-flowing current from the Straits was evident from the speed with which she slid astern of *Minerve*, who had backed her mizen topsail. Hardy stood erect, his gaze on the white-veined waves ahead.

"Who was it?" he growled at the man pulling the stroke oar.

"Cottrell, sir. Fell orf the tops'l yard."

"Can he swim?"

"Dunno, sir."

43

The odds were against it; less than half the men in the Fleet were swimmers. But if he was afloat Cottrell should be easy to sight in this light chop. He lifted his eyes for a moment and saw the leading enemy ship, the frigate, already hull-up even from his low position and dead ahead on the jolly-boat's course, coming up fast under a press of sail. If he held on much longer —but there was no need. Allowing generous time and distance, Cottrell couldn't be farther astern of *Minerve* than this, and a close scanning of the grey troughs and crests all round him revealed no floating object. If Cottrell couldn't swim he must have drowned by now—and the enemy frigate's sails were growing momently against the sky. He turned towards the distant *Minerve* and signalled a negative with his arm sweeping horizontally; Cockburn's glass would be trained on the boat.

"All right, my lads, we'll put about. Pull starboard. Give way together, hard as you can pull."

The strength of the current made itself felt now that they were striving against it. *Minerve*, with loosed sheets and mizen topsail backed, was almost motionless but they were creeping up to her very slowly. Too slowly.

"Pull! Put your backs into it or we'll all see the inside of a Spanish jail."

The men were gasping and straining at the oars. But now the Spanish frigate was hardly a mile astern, a big frigate, of forty guns probably, and he could see the upper sails of the line-of-battle ship beyond her. Any minute now Cockburn would have to run for it.

"Pull!—Pull!"

It was no use. They were still three cable-lengths from *Minerve* and it was obvious that the Spaniard would have her within range long before they could reach her. With relief rather than despondency he saw the flutter and tautening of her canvas as she prepared to sail on, leaving him to the mercies of the Dons; a second lieutenant and a jolly-boat were of negligible value compared to a 40-gun frigate with a commodore and two important passengers on board. But almost at once her sails emptied of wind and her mizen topsail was backed again.

Hardy swore beneath his breath. Impossible—surely Cockburn was not such a fool. He looked astern, and caught his breath in amazement. The Spanish frigate was shortening sail and turning into the wind. She was going to wait for the line-of-battle ship to come up before engaging; her captain must be a bigger fool than Cockburn. He urged his crew to their utmost effort and in five minutes they were under *Minerve*'s quarter. Even as he clambered up to the deck the falls were being made fast to the jolly-boat and the frigate was beginning to gather way, while Culverhouse sent the hands aloft to set studding-sails.

The Commodore was steadying his glass on the poop rail to watch the larger ship, two miles away, coming up to join the waiting frigate which was now fast falling astern of them. Captain Cockburn came to meet Hardy, holding his hat in one hand and dabbing at his brow with a silk handkerchief.

"Too close a thing for my liking, Hardy," he said. "I can only think the Dons suspected a trap—seeing us waiting for 'em they took it we'd a supporting squadron handy."

"Well, thankee, sir," Hardy said grudgingly. "If I'd had the command," he could not forbear adding, "I wouldn't have taken the risk."

Cockburn stared at him for a moment. Then—"No more would I, Hardy," he said abruptly, and walked away.

It seemed a meaningless comment, but later that day over wine and biscuits in the wardroom Hardy heard the first lieutenant's explanation of it.

"Why, the captain left it till the last minute, as we all could see," Culverhouse told him. "He gave the order to bring her on the wind, and I for one thought he was too late even so. Then up comes Commodore Nelson. 'By God,' says he, 'I'll not lose Hardy! Back that mizen tops'l, Captain Cockburn!' So Dandy George does as he's told. I take it you'd rather be here than on your way back to a Spanish prison," he added drily.

"Yes, sure," said Hardy slowly. "But it was a rank imprudence all the same. In my opinion Commodore Nelson won't last long."

"And why not, pray?"

"He's too soft for a sea-officer," said Hardy.

2

Among *Minerve*'s crew of three hundred there were many who believed that an angel had been specially deputed to watch over the frigate during the twenty-four hours from noon on February 11th to noon on the 12th. By something like a miracle she had escaped capture when she delayed to pick up the jolly-boat, and her second escape that same night was miraculous indeed; though Lieutenant Hardy always attributed it to a combination of discipline and seamanship, being convinced that such a combination was more effective than any miracle.

At nightfall on the 11th the last wan bars of sunset vanished behind a wall of fog. The wind, though fair, being light, and Commodore Nelson in a hurry, *Minerve* sped on under a press of sail into fog and darkness. A little after midnight the two hands on lookout right up in the bows let out a simultaneous yell, one asserting that there was land dead ahead and the other more accurately that it was a ship. Hardy, who had the middle watch, had the helm put over at once and ran for'ard. He was in time to see the dark bulk that loomed on the starboard bow, a ship undoubtedly but as huge as a cliff, before the frigate drew away into the cover of the fog. It was impossible that they could have intercepted Admiral Jervis's fleet so soon; on the other hand the departure time of the Spanish fleet from Algeciras Bay, notified to *Minerve* when she called at Gibraltar, could place them in about this position. Hardy had the frigate brought on her course again and posted a line of hands along the deck to pass messages from the lookouts, promising a dozen lashes to any man who spoke above a murmur. The captain and the commodore had come up to the quarterdeck before he finished this swift reorganisation and as he made his report the loud clanging of a bell sounded in the fog on the larboard bow. This time they passed so close to a great ship that she could be made out to be a three-decker and the voices of those on board could be heard.

Cockburn ordered the hands sent to quarters. No guns were run out and no voices raised. When, a few minutes later, *Minerve* passed between two more vast wallowing shapes a pistol-shot on either beam there was no doubt in anyone's mind that she was in the midst of the Spanish fleet.

For three hours, until the middle watch was almost over, *Minerve* steered a tortuous course through night and fog, dodging to leeward at intervals to avoid a Spanish line-of-battle ship. Cockburn had reduced sail to lessen the risk of collision, but even so the frigate's speed was considerably greater than that of the big vessels she was overtaking, who were moving very slowly under just enough canvas to give them steerage way; a three-decker of 112 guns—and the Spaniards had half-a-dozen of them—had nothing like the manoeuvring quality of a frigate in emergency and prudence dictated this speed in a fog. Either for the same reason or by accident, the fleet seemed to be strung out in an irregular line over ten or twelve miles of sea. It was impossible to make any useful estimate of their numbers, but Hardy counted fourteen vessels sighted. Since they were visible from *Minerve* she must of course be visible from them, and the marvel was that not once was she hailed or challenged. There would be frigates accompanying the Spaniards, and it would be easy enough (easier for a Spanish captain than a British, thought Hardy contemptuously) to assume that the frigate forging so recklessly through the fog-shrouded fleet was one of their own ships on some urgent mission. The unlikely reality would hardly enter their heads.

Whatever the reason, *Minerve* passed through unscathed. The pale glimmer of daylight, slowly penetrating the blanket of vapour, found her ship's company still alert and tense but with no ship sighted for the past half-hour. Another half-hour and the fog opened before her bows and shredded away astern, revealing a grey and empty sea. Captain Cockburn spread his studding-sails again and sent all hands below except the watch-on-deck, remaining on the quarterdeck himself with Lieutenant Culverhouse. Hardy, chilled and stiff from the long hours of vigilance, was about to go down to the wardroom when he was accosted by the Commodore. Nelson's thin face was blue with cold; he had not left the deck throughout the middle watch.

"I've bespoke hot coffee, Mr Hardy," he said with chattering teeth. "I hope you'll join Colonel Drinkwater and myself in the day cabin."

"Thankee, sir."

Captain Cockburn's day cabin was right aft beneath the quarterdeck, ranged with his dining cabin and two night cabins across *Minerve*'s forty-foot beam. Measuring fourteen feet by twelve with a height of six feet to the deckhead, it was a small apartment by shore standards though palatial in comparison with the six-foot cube of the lieutenant's cabin. It was empty when they entered. Nelson collapsed wearily on the cushioned bench below the stern windows, through which filtered enough of the pale morning light to make it unnecessary to light the hanging lantern. His body huddled limply there looking strangely shrunken and his angular features drawn and old. This is a sick man, thought Hardy suddenly. The Commodore's quick eye interpreted his glance.

"A touch of fever," he said with a faint smile. "It's seventeen years since the Nicaraguan expedition but the effects are with me still."

"Then by'r leave, sir, it was nonsensical to stay so long on deck," said Hardy bluntly.

The faint smile vanished. Nelson stiffened in his seat, a scowl gathering on his brow and his lower lip jutting angrily. *Don't cross his hawse, because he's never wrong*; Hardy remembered Culverhouse's advice too late. The entrance of Captain Cockburn's steward with a steaming jug and three mugs on a tray saved him from the threatened reprimand. Nelson gulped his coffee avidly and cradled the mug lovingly in his clawlike hands; the dim light showed the scowl gone and a tinge of colour returning to his face.

"You and I, Mr Hardy," he said evenly when the steward had gone, "have a vastly easier lot than the hands on the lower deck, as witness this coffee and these cushioned seats. Yet they're men like ourselves. For them there's no excuse, be it fever or an ague, when their duty calls them aloft to reef tops'ls. I don't choose to be less active in my duty than they are. You take my meaning?"

In Hardy's opinion there was no perceptible likeness between a lower-deck seaman and a commodore, nor was it part of a commodore's duty to spend four hours on deck on a cold and foggy night. But he kept his opinions to himself.

"Yes, sir," he mumbled, and drank coffee.

Colonel Drinkwater came into the cabin, his large leather-bound notebook under his arm. He had come on deck several times during the passage through the Spanish fleet, retiring to his cabin presumably to write down his impressions. He bade the others good morning, poured himself a mug of coffee, and began to discuss the night's events with the commodore, who had brightened preceptibly at sight of the notebook. Hardy sat silent and smouldering. His anger was always slow to rise and now he was angry with himself for voicing what was in effect a reproval of his senior officer, on an impulse he was unable to understand. Nelson's reply had irritated him, too; it implied that the lieutenant didn't understand the men under his command.

"What impressed me most," Drinkwater was saying, "was the discipline of our seamen. When we sheered so close to that big Spanisher I distinctly heard a voice say *'Ponga quatro cubiertos'*—we were in easy earshot, in fact, and a word in English would have given us away. Yet no man in this vessel raised his voice, then or later."

"The British seaman is a fine fellow," said Nelson. "He knows his duty." He turned to Hardy with the evident intention of bringing him into the conversation. "You agree, Mr Hardy, of course."

"He knows what common sense is anyway," said Hardy gruffly. "If he doesn't know it when he joins it's flogged into him quick enough."

"You believe in the efficacy of the cat, I perceive," the colonel said suavely.

"I do, sir."

Hardy glanced sideways at the Commodore. Some imp of perversity was tempting him to show himself harsh and unfeeling.

"I'd have seen to it that any man who raised his voice got a dozen with the cat," he went on, "and every one of 'em knew it."

Drinkwater raised his eyebrows. "The lash is used in the army, of course. But not, I think, nearly to the extent it is in the navy. Indeed, I've heard John Moore—Major-General Moore—advocate its discontinuance."

"I'd support his advocacy, Drinkwater," said Nelson eagerly, thumping his fist on the table. "We should offer the prize, not the punishment—honour and glory, not flogging. By God, if their lordships at the Admiralty issued an order forbidding the use of the cat—"

"They'd deliver England into the hands of the French," Hardy interrupted brusquely.

He saw the Commodore's eye flash and his face darken, but Colonel Drinkwater forestalled any utterance of Nelson's.

"Oh come now, Mr Hardy—an exaggeration, surely."

"Not the least, sir. Look, now. Here's Admiral Jervis with a fleet numbering a dozen-and-a-half of the line, if that many, seeking battle with the Dons. They may have twice as many ships for all we know. Sir John's expected to beat them—and beat them he will, sir."

Nelson's instant nod of approval told Hardy that his rude interruption was, for the moment, forgiven.

"Why will he beat them?" he pursued, unwontedly loquacious. "Because every man aboard his ships is a fighting seaman ready to do his duty—as the commodore says. And what made him so? The cat."

"I don't agree," began the colonel.

"England depends absolutely upon the Navy," Hardy plodded on remorselessly, "and the Navy depends on gunners and topmen who'll obey an order on the instant and obey it with skill and courage. What are we given for gunners and topmen? Why, landsmen and jailbirds, thieves, drunkards, vagabonds—the dregs of England, colonel. Half of 'em are more beasts than men. D'ye think they care tuppence for honour and glory?"

Drinkwater looked thoughtful. "I see the point you're making, Mr Hardy. All the same—"

"I take leave to doubt that, Hardy," Nelson said sharply. "'Aft the more profit, for'ard the greater honour'—that's a lower-deck proverb you must have heard."

"Aye, sir. That's when we've made men of them, with the cat to help us." Hardy addressed Drinkwater again. "Many a Navy ship puts to sea with a dozen prime seamen and the rest the poor beasts I spoke of. In a day, two days, she may have to fight for her life against the French or a storm. The beasts have to be turned into men in a damned short time, colonel, and I see no other way but the Navy's way. Show them their duty, order them to do it, let them learn at once that if they don't or won't they'll be flogged."

"And if they can't do it?" frowned the colonel.

"There's a lot of men don't know what they can do until the alternative's a flogging. I don't deny it's a hard way. But it makes men. Maybe there'll come a time when we can throw the cat overboard, but it'll be a different Navy, and a different England too, when that—"

Hardy's deep voice tailed away. He looked from colonel to commodore in some embarrassment and lowered his eyes.

"Beg pardon, gentlemen," he mumbled. "I fancy I'm talking too much."

Nelson, who had been studying him intently, smiled suddenly. "And that," he said, "must be a rare occurrence. I believe we have been instructed—eh, colonel?"

"But not in humanity," said Drinkwater coldly.

"Captain Cockburn was writing a letter when I entered his cabin yesterday," Nelson said with apparent irrelevance. "It was to the widow of the man who was lost overboard—Cottrell. He told me that it was at the instance—'the damned persistent pestering' was his own phrase—of his second lieutenant."

Hardy's large face took on a slowly-deepening crimson. He rose to his feet and picked up his hat from the bench.

"I trust you'll excuse me, sir," he said woodenly. "I have a class of midshipmen to instruct."

He left the day cabin, by no means sure that he hadn't made a fool of himself. He was dimly conscious of valuing Commodore Nelson's good opinion while not giving a damn for Colonel Drinkwater's.

All next day *Minerve* drove on her course, nor'-west by west, heading for the rendezvous with the Fleet twenty leagues off Cape St Vincent. Nothing more was seen of the Spanish ships. The strong Levanter that still blew might well have set them far to westward. On the morning of February 13th the upper sails of Admiral Jervis's ships were sighted and some hours later (the easterly wind having died away to a fitful breeze) the frigate was exchanging signals with Sir John's flagship, *Victory*. Commodore Nelson carried his news of their passage through the Spanish fleet to the admiral, including Lieutenant Hardy's estimate that they numbered fourteen at the very least and twenty or more at a fair guess, and thereafter shifted his flag into his old ship *Captain*, 74. The frigate *Lively* was to have borne the ex-Viceroy of Corsica and Colonel Drinkwater to England without delay and the two were transferred to her; but at Sir Gilbert's earnest request that he might stay and "assist at a general action of the British Fleet" the admiral postponed her departure.

Three of Jervis's five frigates were dispatched to seek the Spaniards and bring warning of their approach. And at 5.30 in the morning of February 14th, St Valentine's Day, the *Niger* frigate brought the news that the Spanish fleet was ten miles to windward on a course east-south-east. Three hours later the low-lying mist of a sunless morning with little wind lifted to reveal a long straggling line of great ships, twenty-seven of them to Jervis's fifteen.

3

"Just bloody beaters, that's all we are," grumbled Lieutenant Culverhouse. "Flush all these fat partridges and then stand back for our betters to shoot 'em."

"If they ever get near enough," returned Lieutenant Hardy.

The two were standing at *Minerve*'s lee rail watching the British line of battle ahead on the starboard bow. Across the quarterdeck Captain Cockburn, exercising his prerogative of having the weather side to himself, was also watching intently.

Like the four frigates sailing in close company with her, *Minerve* was creeping over the smooth water under topsails and topgallants, her decks cleared for action but her gunports closed. It was a little after six bells of the forenoon watch, two hours since the first clear sighting of the Spanish fleet.

Hardy could understand Culverhouse's frustration but he considered his complaint absurd. The duty of the frigates attached to the opposing battle-fleets was to bring the fleets together; thereafter they would lie off in readiness to assist any disabled ship that needed to be towed out of the mêlée. To Hardy's mind they resembled the squires in the mediaeval battles, who had stay out of the fighting unless the knight they served was unhorsed and had to be dragged to safety. A mediaeval battle, he reflected, would have been joined long before this. He put his glass to his eye and swept it slowly across the southern horizon. The Spanish fleet made a shocking sight for a sea-officer's eye. In marked contrast to the fifteen British ships, all close-hauled in perfect line ahead with Troubridge's *Culloden* leading, the Spaniards seemed to be bunched anyhow, the only distinctive formation being a division (probably by accident, thought Hardy) into two groups of ships with a considerable gap between them. What wind there was blew from west-sou'-west and they had it almost astern, whereas the British line, approaching nearly at right-angles to their course, had it for'ard of the starboard beam. Thus the smaller group of Spaniards was passing to leeward and the larger from windward. *Culloden* was heading straight for the gap.

"For God's sake whistle up a wind, Hardy," said Culverhouse impatiently.

The breeze, blowing fitfully across a leaden sea under the low motionless clouds, was so light that the ships of the line had not yet furled their main courses, and even so they were only moving at a walking pace. It was not often that Hardy's thoughts turned to Susan Manfield but he recalled now something she had said about the excitement a sea-officer must feel when his ship "dashed into battle at top speed with the guns banging and the men cheering." This interminable crawl wouldn't have suited Susan.

It was possible to see the Spanish ships clearly without the glass now. The leeward group seemed to be turning, presenting their sterns. Twenty-one ships were in the windward group and one of them was a gigantic vessel—she must be the *Santissima Trinidada*, the biggest ship in the world. He caught sight of a flutter of bunting at the yardarm of the seventh ship in the British line, *Victory*. Jervis was probably confirming his intention of breaking the enemy line—he'd be missing a chance if he didn't go through it and turn to windward. Half-past eleven, his watch told him. As he returned it to his fob Cockburn snapped an order at the helmsman and another at his lieutenants. *Minerve* was fore-reaching on her companions and sheets were eased off to spill wind from her tops'ls. The five frigates were sailing parallel with the rear ships of the line—*Captain*, *Diadem*, and *Excellent*—and half-a-mile to windward of them, *Lively* in advance of the others. In a little while now, Hardy reflected as he returned to the lee rail with Culverhouse, Colonel Drinkwater would have something to write in his notebook. He lifted his glass and squinted through it at *Captain*, broad on *Minerve*'s beam and last but two in the line. Her double row of gunports were open and her quarterdeck was populous with blue coats and the red of the marines. He could see Commodore Nelson plainly, walking slowly up and down with a lanky figure who must be Captain Miller. Hardy frowned. It was nonsensical to feel a twinge of apprehension, but he couldn't help it. The impression he had formed of Horatio Nelson was of a man who had an overwhelming faith in his own judgement and would act upon it without hesitation; and in Hardy's opinion this was not the sort of man who should be serving under Admiral Sir John Jervis, who spared no one who deviated from his own rigid ideas of discipline.

"*Culloden*'s opened fire!" exclaimed Culverhouse, whose glass was on the British van.

The detonations of Troubridge's broadside sounded as he spoke the last word and the answering Spanish fire merged with them. The spreading clouds of smoke made it difficult to see what was happening in detail, and as ship after ship followed *Culloden* and the engagement became more general Hardy found it impossible to discern precisely which vessels were in action. The faltering wind, besides causing each ship unconscionable delay in arriving within range, allowed the powder-smoke to lie in billowing masses through which only the bright orange flicker of gunfire and an occasional spar or flag could be seen. The din of the guns became slowly louder and more continuous. *Prince George, Orion,* and *Colossus* were certainly in the thick of it with *Culloden*—three 74's and a 98-gun ship. *Blenheim*, another 98, was opening fire when Hardy had to interrupt his observation. Lord Garlies, in command of *Lively* and senior captain of the frigate squadron, was signalling. *Heave-to*. The frigates came slowly round to the wind and backed their mizen topsails. When he was able to give his attention to the battle again Hardy's mystification at this unexpected order was removed. Garlies had been quick to perceive a change in battle tactics and was waiting to see which direction the slow-moving fleets would take.

Breaking through the wide gap, *Culloden* and her followers had crossed the bows of the foremost Spanish ships of the big windward group to engage them from the other side; and the Spanish admiral (Cordova, Hardy remembered) was countering this manoeuvre by turning, with all his leading ships, across the wind to head northwards, so that the vessels of the Spanish van were beginning to appear on the farther side of the British line moving parallel to it in the opposite direction. *Victory*'s signal—'All ships tack in succession'—was being obeyed by *Culloden* and the first ships of the van were following in a full turn, firing now with their larboard guns and receiving the thunderous Spanish broadsides in return. A glance to leeward showed him the vessels of Cordova's fleet that had been cut off from the rest. With one exception they were drifting in apparent confusion, unable to beat back against the wind; if they got into action at all it would only be late in the day. The exception, a big three-decker, was close-hauled and making slowly towards the British centre.

A seaman trotted up to the belfry on the poop and struck four double clangs from the bell. Eight bells—noon. Still the heavy layers of smoke hid the only five British ships that had achieved contact with the enemy. The other ten, rigidly in line, were following each other to the point where *Culloden* had made her 180-degree turn. Hardy knew that the Admiral regarded this traditional maintenance of the line as essential in a fleet engagement, but he began to wonder whether it might not lose its effectiveness in the present circumstances.

"Hands to make sail! Main courses, there!"

Lively had made the signal for independent action. The frigates separated, their greater speed enabling them to range up and down in search of opportunities for rendering service. Cockburn, tacking *Minerve* to windward to close the British centre, found his opportunity within a few minutes. Out from the dun smoke-cloud drifted the 74-gun *Colossus*, her sails in tatters and her foresail yard shot away. Astern of her the *Irresistible*, in the act of tacking, swerved to avoid collision and narrowly escaped being rammed by *Victory*, next astern. The flagship backed her topsail and the *Colossus* floundered out of the line, in stays and unable to get steerage way. *Minerve* crept under her quarter and Cockburn hailed her, suggesting that *Minerve* should tow her back into the line, but the offer was peremptorily declined. Her larboard flank was holed and splintered and most of her rail shot away; there was some justification for Culverhouse's remark that she'd had a bellyful. *Minerve* had barely sheered away on the starboard tack when she found herself crossing the bows of the three-decker that had come up from the Spanish leeward division. They passed so close that Hardy could make out her name in gold scroll-work—*Principe d'Asturias*—but no shots were exchanged; no frigate would challenge a 112-gun ship and the Spaniard's 32-pounders were loaded for larger prey. She was making for *Victory*, like herself a three-decker and of almost equal gun-power. Gazing astern as *Minerve* sailed clear, the officers on the frigate's quarterdeck had a plain view of the encounter.

The Spanish ship held on her course until it seemed that she must collide with *Victory* bow-to-bow. One or other must give way. When she was within a pistol-shot of the flagship the Spaniard lost his nerve and put the helm hard down, turning his ship to larboard. The men at her starboard guns were no doubt taken by surprise, for only a few guns of her broadside fired. As she continued her turn she presented an open target for *Victory* and half-a-hundred cannon flamed and roared at close range.

"Look—look, by God!" yelled Culverhouse, positively leaping up and down at Hardy's side. "Her helm's shot away!"

The *Principe d'Asturias*, her upper deck a shambles and her rudder jammed, continued to swing slowly round until she had made a full circle. *Victory*'s gunners had reloaded by the time the unhappy ship, unable to help herself, was again close before their muzzles. The second devastating broadside smashed into her. With all three topmasts shot away and not a man left standing on her deck, the *Principe d'Asturias* drifted helplessly to leeward and out of the fight.

Minerve was running northward with the light breeze over her larboard quarter, passing in turn the rear ships of the British line on their southward course. Through the gaps between the huge slow-moving hulls Hardy could see the flame-shot smoke of the fight that was raging half-a-mile away but it was impossible to tell how the battle was going. Captain Cockburn, who was standing with the two lieutenants at the weather rail, smote fist into palm impatiently.

"Two hours gone since *Culloden* opened the ball," he said, "and only six of ours engaged. At this rate Jervis'll never get his crushing victory."

Hardy looked at his watch and was surprised to find that it was already after half-past one. The February afternoon, cloudy and sunless as the morning, would darken quickly at the approach of evening.

"What's more," Cockburn added, a note of anxiety in his voice, "Cordova's winning the weather-gauge. He'll soon be able to cross astern of *Excellent*."

Culverhouse levelled his glass. "And that's what he's about, sir. They're altering course, easterly. They could come down on our rear from windward—or they could hold on and get clear of us."

It was true, Hardy saw. *Minerve* had passed *Captain* and *Diadem* and was about to pass *Excellent*, the rearmost ship of the southward-heading seven that had yet to make the turn. Beyond *Excellent*'s stern he could see the half-dozen Spanish ships that were not hidden by the rolling smoke of conflict. Jervis's last order, signalled nearly two hours ago, had now brought the British battle-line into a V-shaped formation, and Cordova was heading to cross its extremities. *Victory*, somewhere in the smoke and uproar of the fight, could not have observed this move nor could any signal she might make be seen. Unless those leading Spanish ships could be intercepted Admiral Juan de Cordova would most likely use his advantage to run eastward under all the sail he could cram on and rejoin his leeward division. And if he eluded a full battle now the chance of a crushing blow at Spanish sea-power would be gone.

"One of the line's wearing, by God!" Cockburn shouted excitedly. "That's Nelson, or I'm a Dutchman!"

Captain was bearing round away from the wind, leaving her place in the line. She made her turn and passed through the gap between *Diadem* and *Excellent* to head straight for the Spanish van.

Of the three men who watched eagerly from *Minerve*'s quarterdeck two were enthusiastic; the peril they had observed was probably going to be averted. The third was both disapproving and apprehensive. Hardy knew well that for a commodore to change the plan of battle without orders from the admiral-in-command was unforgivable. Nelson had disobeyed Jervis's signal for all ships to tack in succession; it needed only a lucky shot from one of the Spanish ships, dismasting *Captain* and leaving her helpless, to make his court-martial and disgrace certain. It could even be worse than that. Disobeying orders in a vital fleet engagement was at least as great a crime as failing to do one's utmost in the face of the enemy, and for the latter offence a rear-admiral, John Byng, had been condemned to death and shot only forty years ago. Hardy's heavy red brows were drawn together in a scowl as he steadied his glass on the errant 74.

It did not ease his anxiety to perceive that the three leading Spanish ships, towards which *Captain* was steering, were all massive three-deckers. One of them, he was fairly sure, was the gigantic *Santissima Trinidada*, carrying nearly twice *Captain*'s weight of guns. He found himself letting out pent breath in relief when he saw above the billowing smoke on the left the upper masts and flags of a British ship moving to the attack—*Culloden*, probably—and caught sight of *Excellent* bearing away from the line to follow *Captain*. Cuthbert Collingwood, *Excellent*'s captain, was an old shipmate of Horatio Nelson's and was evidently prepared to risk his career for his friend's sake.

The 74 was almost into the Spanish line now. A vast eruption of smoke and flame seemed to swallow her up and she passed from sight, *Excellent* following her into the flame and smother a few minutes later. And there ended, for Lieutenant Hardy, his actual witnessing of the Battle of Cape St Vincent.

For three hours the British frigates, hovering on the fringe of the fight, caught only occasional glimpses of the confused struggle that was spread over a square mile of sea. The failing breeze blowing from beyond the warring ships sent dense clouds of dun-coloured smoke billowing across the whole area, and from inside the clouds came the unceasing crash of gunfire. On the grey sea outside the canopy of smoke were only the five frigates, the disabled *Colossus*, and the distant sails of a few Spanish vessels hull-down in the west.

From time to time wreckage drifted out from beneath the dun curtain, fragments of woodwork and broken spars, sometimes with men clinging to them. *Minerve*'s jolly-boat picked up three Spanish seamen, two of them badly wounded and all of them shocked and deaf from the detonations of the guns. Culverhouse's questions could get no sense out of them. By five o'clock the short February day was waning and the gunfire was slackening and becoming sporadic. Out of the thinning cloud huge shapes emerged by degrees, shapes that had once been tall ships. Now they were dishevelled hulks, shattered and shot-torn, half of them dismasted and all of them with such sails as were left holed and rent in a score of places. The desultory firing ceased and voices screeched distantly in a triple British cheer. As *Minerve* closed the disorderly mass of stricken vessels it was possible to see that none of them wore Spanish colours.

"There's *Captain*," Cockburn said curtly.

Hardy had already marked the 74 and was examining her through his glass. She looked a complete wreck, all three masts gone by the board and her hull gashed and splintered. Knowing what a storm of enemy shot must have brought her to that state he could guess at the heavy casualties among her crew. It seemed likely enough that a commodore in a conspicuous uniform, with no notion of prudence, was among them. He surprised himself by having to gulp down some emotion at the thought, and was glad when Cockburn's order to have the boat lowered gave him something to do.

"I'm proposing to take *Captain* in tow if Miller agrees,"

said Cockburn. "She can't hoist a rag of sail on those stumps. I'm sending Midshipman Bradley in charge of the boat—"

"I'll go, sir," said Hardy quickly.

The captain regarded him with some surprise. "You'll see to the rousing-out of our cable, Mr Hardy, if you please. Mr Bradley is capable of taking a message, I should hope."

Minerve's boat was away for some time. Hardy, his towing-cable on deck and ready for passing, was back on the quarter-deck when she returned with a pale-faced but wildly-excited Midshipman Bradley whose report was somewhat incoherent. His delay in returning was because Commodore Nelson had asked to be taken on board *Irresistible*. (Hardy suppressed a sigh of relief.) A sight to see, was the Commodore—clothes in tatters, face black with powder, all the crown of his hat shot away. And *Captain*'s decks were an awful sight, all blood and bodies. Sixty killed, she'd had. But it'd been a great victory, all the Dons that hadn't run smashed to splinters and four of 'em prizes—

"Does Captain Miller want a tow or doesn't he?" snapped Cockburn.

"Oh—yes, sir. We've brought the line aboard. And sir—we brought one of *Captain*'s officers back with us, Lieutenant Withers. He's wounded, arm and head, and Captain Miller's compliments, sir, and he'd be obliged if you'd find a berth for him, there being no cabins left to speak of in his own ship."

"Well, he's damned lucky to have any ship left to speak of," said Cockburn.

Two hours later, with the last light of day fading in the gloomy west, *Minerve* and her charge were lying hove-to to leeward of the long British line. Admiral Jervis had signalled all ships to form line and heave-to for the night; shattered as they were, incapable indeed of further battle or pursuit, each vessel had contrived, by her own efforts or with the aid of a tow from a frigate, to take station. Far away in the gathering darkness the surviving Spanish ships were huddled like sheep awaiting the onslaught of wolves. But the wolves were as powerless to attack as the sheep to escape.

Withers, third lieutenant of the *Captain*, had been accommodated in Captain Cockburn's spare night cabin, where Perry, *Minerve*'s surgeon, had dressed his wounds and made him reasonably comfortable. Perry had great faith in the efficacy of wine when lost blood needed replacing (in the case of Perry himself, a full-blooded man, other excuses were forthcoming) and it was probably a sufficiency of wine that lubricated Withers's tongue when Hardy visited him that evening.

"I've never seen anything like it, Mr Hardy," said Withers. "And I don't want to see anything like it again, or not when I'm in among it myself."

He was a stocky man of middle age who—as he had told Hardy—had reached the quarterdeck by way of the hawsehole. What could be seen of his face under the swathing bandages was brown and deeply lined, and his mouth had a sullen twist to it. A boarding-pike had grazed his arm, and the more serious cut across his scalp had been made by a Spanish officer's sword.

"*Captain* stopped 'em from running for it, at any rate," said Hardy.

Withers snorted. "Maybe so, maybe not. *Culloden*'s guns had done the trick already, I reckon. Troubridge had crammed on all sail and was pushing through the Dons like a whirlwind, d'ye see, and the broadside he gave the *San Nicolas* shoved her up against *San Josef* with a wallop that snapped her topmasts like twigs. He could have made prize of one or t'other, but does he? No—slams on to engage that whopper, the *Trinidada*. *Blenheim* was hammering away at her too. That was when we came up."

"The Commodore was giving the orders, eh?"

"He was," said Withers with emphasis. "Screeching 'em, like a madman. Laid us on board *Josef* and *Nicolas* both, with *Trinidada*'s broadside on our beam for good measure

Slam—bang—down comes our foretopmast, helm shot away, half the hands on deck killed and half the rest wounded, not a sail or a shroud left. Our spritsail yard was hooked in the mizen rigging of the *Nicolas*. 'Away boarders!' yells the Commodore. He jumps up into the mizen chains. 'Come on!' he screeches. 'Westminster Abbey or glorious victory!'"

"Did he say that?" asked Hardy incredulously.

"I heard him. More like 'glorious victory or dismissed the service,' thinks I. But mind you," Withers added, "I didn't think like that at the time. None of us who followed him stopped to think, I reckon."

"You boarded with him, Mr Withers?"

Withers raised his unbandaged arm and scratched the side of his face reflectively. "It's funny thing, Mr Hardy, but I couldn't *not* follow him, if you see what I mean. It's something about him. Sets you a bit above yourself. The hands felt it too—they were clambering along the spritsail yard, cheering themselves hoarse. But it was Captain Berry I followed in the end, because one of the redcoats smashed in the quarter-gallery window of the *Nicolas* and Nelson ducked in that way. The others of us swarmed up over the rail—I got a graze with a pike before I pistolled the man who held it—and a bash on the crown while we were fighting our way to the poop."

"The Dons showed plenty of fight, then?"

"Half-a-minute of swashing and then 'mercy, mercy!' Do 'em justice, though, they'd very few men fit to fight. Captain Berry and I took three Spanish officers prisoner and they handed over their swords to the captain. Nelson, who'd boarded through the after cabins, came up on the quarterdeck just as we were hauling down the Spanish colours. If you'd pass me that glass of wine, Mr Hardy, I'd be obliged. All this talk is making me dry."

Having refreshed himself, the lieutenant continued his story. The *San Nicolas* was tightly jammed against the stern of the larger *San Josef*, a first-rate of 112 guns, whose stern-gallery overhung the smaller ship's quarterdeck. Pistols were being fired from the gallery windows and Nelson ordered some soldiers of the 69th regiment, who were serving as marines, to return the fire, at the same time calling on the seamen from *Captain* to board the *San Josef*. At this moment, however, the pistol-shots ceased and a Spanish officer looked over the rail and shouted that the *San Josef* surrendered.

"So up we go," said Withers, "and there's the Spanish captain with Admiral Winthuysen's sword, which the admiral can't surrender himself because both his legs are shot off, and a couple of other Dons with swords to surrender. Nelson shakes hands with the captain and hands the swords to a seaman to tuck under his arm. That's as much as I know of it," he finished, "because I went into a swoon that instant. Loss of blood, I reckon."

"Well, I'll take leave to congratulate you, Mr Withers," Hardy said. "*Captain*'s part in this action will make a stir in England, or I am much mistaken."

Lieutenant Withers's hard grey eyes regarded him without enthusiasm. "There's two or three score of her men who won't stir till the trump of doom. I hope the Commodore's ready to answer for them."

"Oh come, now!" Hardy protested. "Commodore Nelson saw where his duty lay and took his ship thither. I'd have done the same, I hope."

"You wouldn't have taken us under the guns of three first-rates, Mr Hardy. It wasn't necessary, y'know."

"The Commodore risked more than anyone. That took a deal of courage."

"I grant you that," Withers said grudgingly. "I never saw a man show less fear in a fight."

Hardy was silent for a moment, wondering why he felt bound to defend Nelson against all criticism now.

"Only three days ago," he muttered to himself, "I said he was too soft for a sea-officer."

Withers heard him. "If he's soft at all," he said, "it's in the head."

4

Lieutenant Hardy had not overstated the case when he remarked that the victory of Cape St Vincent would make a stir in England. Mr Pitt's crumbling government, saved at the eleventh hour, was grateful. There was an earldom for Jervis, baronetcies for his two vice-admirals, and the Order of the Bath (by his own request) for Horatio Nelson, whose promotion by seniority to Rear-Admiral of the Blue had been gazetted before the battle took place. The thanks of both Houses of Parliament were carried by acclamation and the King sent gold medals to all captains of line-of-battle ships. The Mediterranean Fleet did not hear of all this until the beginning of April, for the *Lively*, carrying home Sir Gilbert Elliot and Colonel Drinkwater and the tidings of victory, arrived in Spithead on March 3rd; but enough Fleet gossip had reached Hardy's ears to prepare him for the wave of popular acclaim that had made the hitherto unknown name of Nelson almost a household word.

Shipboard rumour was not a thing that Hardy customarily took notice of. But an odd mixture of interest and anxiety made him prick up his ears when Nelson's name was mentioned, and he could hardly help piecing together a story whose sources were unimpeachable even if (to his mind) it threw little credit on its subject. Even before *Lively* sailed from Lagos Bay on the Algarve coast, whither Jervis took his ships and the four prizes after the battle, Culverhouse (who had dined on board with her first lieutenant) brought back one part of the tale, and various ship-visits during the weeks of refitting in Lisbon harbour produced others. The later *Gazettes* and letters from England went some way towards persuading a disapproving Hardy that Rear-Admiral Sir Horatio Nelson, K.B., so far from being soft in the head, was in some ways as hardheaded as the next man.

On the evening after the battle, it appeared, Nelson had gone straight on board the flagship without stopping to change into a clean uniform or wash his powder-blackened face, to tell his story to the Admiral. It was a wise move (as Hardy conceded) and likely to avert any reprimand Jervis was meditating. Early next morning he had himself rowed to *Lively* and dictated to a willing Drinkwater his own account of *Captain*'s engagement with three Spanish first-rates, which the Colonel undertook to publish after a copy had been sent via Sir Gilbert Elliot to the First Lord of the Admiralty. Proof that the energetic author had lost no time when he got to London arrived with the mails in May—a hundred copies of a best-selling booklet entitled *A Narrative of the Proceedings of the British Fleet in the Battle off Cape St Vincent, by an Officer of H.M. Land Forces*. Hardy, frowning over the hastily-printed pages, found no difficulty in believing the story of its source. "With a cry of 'Glorious victory or Westminster Abbey,'" Drinkwater wrote, "Commodore Nelson dashed into the Spaniard's chains and was in a moment on board her." And though there was a brief tribute to the "noble support" rendered by Captain Collingwood in *Culloden* the fact that *Blenheim* and *Prince George*, *Orion* and *Culloden* had been in action with the Spanish fleet for nearly three hours before *Captain*'s bold intervention was passed over. Intentionally or not, the impression Colonel Drinkwater conveyed to his readers was that Nelson had won the Battle of Cape St Vincent almost single-handed. The London journals and news-letters seized with glee upon Drinkwater's account, for the official *Gazette* gave them little to descant on. As usual, Admiral Jervis's dispatch was printed in full in the *Gazette*, but it mentioned no names and said nothing whatever about *Captain*'s exploit. It was no surprise to Hardy to learn from subsequent newspapers that Nelson had been made a freeman of London, Bath, and Norwich, having presented one of his captured Spanish swords to the latter city. He had more than a suspicion that the jest of "Nelson's patent bridge for boarding first-rates" which was being bandied about the Fleet had been invented by Nelson.

All this moved Hardy to scorn. Himself a man of rigid personal integrity, he had always disliked the lobbying and currying of favour by which a good many naval officers sought to advance themselves in their career; Nelson's less conventional methods he saw as chicanery of an even lower sort. But his scorn was tempered with other emotions—disappointment and a kind of pity. In judging his fellow-men he gave very high marks to courage, and he could not but admire in Horatio Nelson the special courage of a man of frail body and poor health who overcomes his handicaps to perform heroic deeds. It was the more of a shame, then, that he should prove vain and self-assertive.

There was no doubt, however, that the new Rear-Admiral was in high favour with John Jervis, now Earl of St Vincent. Though he was the junior flag-officer on the station he was appointed to the command of the inshore squadron off Cadiz, a post he found so unexciting that he pressed St Vincent to allow him to attack Cadiz itself and succeeded in setting the city alight in three places with shells from the bomb-ketch *Thunderer*. When the Spaniards unexpectedly sent gunboats and armed launches in an attempt to take the bomb-ketch Nelson sped to her rescue with all the boats he could muster and took part in the hand-to-hand fighting that followed. Again at his own request, he was given a squadron of three 74's and a frigate to try and intercept three Spanish ships laden with gold from Spain's American colonies, an enterprise which met with no success. *Minerve* was the frigate selected, and on the squadron's return to Lisbon Lieutenant Hardy met Nelson for the first time since the shifting of the commodore's flag to *Captain*.

It was the briefest of encounters. The Rear-Admiral had come on board for a word with Captain Cockburn; Hardy was setting the anchor-watch when the two came on deck. Nelson came straight across to him with hand outstretched.

"Mr Hardy, I'm delighted to see you."

"Thankee, Sir Horatio."

"I'm only sorry I've so little time to spare for a friend. I shall study to make amends."

Then he was piped over the side to his waiting barge.

That was all. But the warmth in the glance of that one brilliant eye, the grip of the thin hand, were enough to wipe away the image of the vainglorious self-seeker. Hardy was conscious of a desire to serve under the immediate command of this man who had won his scorn a week or two earlier. Reflecting on this circumstance later, and finding it odd, he could only remember Lieutenant Withers's words and shake his head over them in solemn puzzlement : *it's something about him.*

THREE

1

"To Lieut. T. Masterman Hardy
    of H.M. ship La Minerva   29 May 1797
    You are hereby required and directed to take upon you the charge and command of the French National Corvette La Mutine, *captured by the boats of the* Lively *and* Minerve, *and proceed with her without loss of time to Lisbon, where you will deliver the letters you will herewith receive to Sir John Jervis, K.B., and remain there, keeping charge of the* Mutine, *until you receive his further orders.*
                                                        BEN. HALLOWELL
                                                                     Capt."

It was this letter that first revealed to Lieutenant Hardy that he had an ambition. When Culverhouse was posted to *Colossus*, 74, and Hardy had taken his place as first lieutenant of *Minerve*, he had been more than content with his lot; but Hallowell's letter amounted to an official appointment (subject to the Admiral's confirmation) as commander of *Mutine*, and that made the possibility of attaining post rank a great deal more likely. Of a sudden Lieutenant Hardy perceived that his satisfaction in being first lieutenant of a fine frigate had been illusory. To command a fine frigate himself, with his name on the list of post-captains, was no longer a nonsensical fancy to be shrugged out of his mind but a goal he might reasonably set himself.

Though Hardy had not exchanged a word with Rear-Admiral Sir Horatio Nelson for two months his new command was (in a way) a result of the Rear-Admiral's restless enterprise. Everyone in the Fleet knew that since the battle on St Valentine's Day Nelson had been able to twist Lord St Vincent round his little finger; he had persuaded Jervis to send two frigates to Tenerife to look into Santa Cruz Bay in search of the missing Spanish treasure-ships, which seemed to be something of an obsession with him just now. *Lively* and *Minerve* had accordingly been sent, the former now under the command of Captain Benjamin Hallowell, a post-captain of six years' seniority. Hallowell was Canadian-born, a man as big and as blunt as Hardy himself and an old friend of Horatio Nelson. It was he who had declared, when they found Santa Cruz Bay to contain no treasure-ships but only a large armed brig-sloop, that Old Jarvie should have the brig for a souvenir.

The cutting-out of the *Mutine* by night had been no easy operation. Besides mounting 14 guns and having a complement of 130 men, she lay close in to the quays of Santa Cruz town and under the guns of a redoubt. As senior lieutenant Hardy commanded the boats of the two frigates, and though the boarding-parties succeeded in carrying her after a desperate fight the brig was under fire for two hours before they could tow her out of range, the wind having fallen away to a dead calm. All things considered, the British party were lucky to get off with no men killed and only 15 wounded; the latter included Hardy, who incurred a cutlass-slash across the skull which troubled him for a year afterwards.

Mutine, rated as a corvette in the French Navy, proved to be a valuable prize. She was new-built, fast, armed with twelve long 6-pounders and two 36-pounder carronades, as handy on a wind as a sloop and as staunch in ill weather as any frigate. When in accordance with his orders Hardy took her to Lisbon and delivered Hallowell's dispatches to Lord St Vincent, the old Admiral seized upon her at once to assist his few overworked frigates in their ceaseless patrol of the Biscay ports. Hardy was confirmed in his rank of commander, and with Gage from the *Minerve* as his lieutenant spent the weeks from mid-July to the end of August in independent cruising, keeping an eye on the ports and inlets between Ferrol and Bilbao where sundry units of the French and Spanish fleets were thought to be harboured. Thus it was that he neither took part in the disastrous attack on Santa Cruz nor even heard what had happened until Nelson had sailed for England. A whole year, in fact, was to pass before he saw Nelson again.

On a hazy August morning *Mutine* was heading southward twenty miles off Finisterre when her lookout reported two sail on the starboard bow, a frigate and a ship of the line, which on approach proved to be *Culloden*, 74, with *Emerald* in attendance. Signal flags fluttered from the big ship's yardarm, requiring *Mutine*'s captain to come on board. Five minutes later Hardy was being greeted by Captain Thomas Troubridge on the quarterdeck of *Culloden*. It was the first time the two had met, but Hardy had heard a great deal about Tom Troubridge and none of it to his discredit. He had been a midshipman with Nelson in the West Indies twenty-five years ago, was the son of a baker of Irish descent, and had attained his present position high on the list of post-captains by sheer capacity and courage. Half-a-head shorter than Hardy, he was the same age as Nelson but looked a dozen years younger with his pleasant boyish face and curiously gentle brown eyes.

"Come below till we find a glass of wine, Mr Hardy," Troubridge said; it was his foible to insist on his origins by talking with a marked brogue, though he himself was English born. "Where will you be heading, now?"

"Lisbon, sir, to make my report."

"I'm to join Captain Saumarez's squadron off Corunna." Troubridge led the way into the smaller day cabin and produced bottle and glasses. "You'll have news for me and maybe

I'll have some for you. Have you had any action with the Dons?"

Hardy, sipping excellent Madeira, had little to tell him. He replied briefly that he had taken three prizes, Spanish merchant vessels, and sent them to Lisbon; on the Biscay coast of Spain there seemed to be no sign at all of enemy naval activity. *Culloden*'s captain eyed him thoughtfully over the rim of his glass.

"Would you be expecting to find any, Captain Hardy?"

The courtesy rank, to which he was not really entitled, was evidently intended to put Hardy at his ease and he accepted its indication that this was an informal talk.

"No. It's a nonsensical idea. There's no vessel of force in Santander or Bilbao and a score in Cadiz."

"I agree." Troubridge raised his glass. "And here's to the day they come out of Cadiz again. But it's more likely, in my opinion, that the French will come out of Toulon. They've a baker's dozen of first-rates there. That was Admiral Nelson's opinion also," he added. "I heard him express it before he was sent home."

"Sent home?" repeated Hardy sharply.

"Invalided home," Troubridge amended hastily. "Of course, you'll not have heard of this. His right arm's been amputated above the elbow."

"Lord ha' mercy!" Hardy was shocked from his usual imperturbability. "Lost his right arm, you say? How did that come about?"

"It was at Santa Cruz. You left the Fleet at the beginning of July, I believe? The Expedition sailed on the fifteenth, four of the line and three frigates with Nelson in *Theseus*. I had command of the landing-parties—'General Troubridge' I was dubbed by Sir Horatio. He planned it all, Hardy, from the ammunition each ship would need to the number of rungs on the scaling ladders. It was to be a surprise attack by night—"

Captain Troubridge was at least Irish enough to make the

most of a story. His listener's stolid face wore a slight but deepening frown as the tale of that ill-judged attempt on the island of Tenerife unfolded itself, with Troubridge's uncritical admiration of Horatio Nelson plain in the telling. Though the treasure-ships from Mexico (the original objective of the operation) had not reached Santa Cruz, Nelson had cajoled St Vincent into allowing him to carry out his plan of attack on the port. Two hundred seamen and marines under Troubridge were to land from boats and storm the two batteries on the hillside commanding the harbour, silence the guns, and then descend on the town and summon the Governor to surrender; the 74's would come in to cover the town with their guns as soon as the batteries were taken.

"You'll be knowing Santa Cruz Bay well enough, Hardy," Troubridge interrupted himself to say. "You cut out *Mutine* there."

"Yes," Hardy said shortly. "On the one calm day in a hundred. I'd not care to land boats by night in any other weather."

That was just it, Troubridge went on, looking a trifle dashed. The night landing had failed. Strong winds and unexpected currents had prevented the boats from coming within a mile of land before daylight came. The landing-parties were re-embarked, and gales and cloudy weather kept the squadron at sea off the coast for two days before a second landing was attempted, this time with the Admiral himself in one of the boats. It was to be a direct attack on the town from a landing on the mole in the centre of the bay, ignoring the hillside batteries.

"But scrounch it all!" Hardy broke in, moved by rare emotion to a Dorset expletive. "The Dons knew all about it by now—they'd had three days warning. They were ready for you, sure."

They were ready indeed, Troubridge admitted sadly. The boats, in six divisions and carrying seven hundred men, had pulled for ninety minutes against wind and stinging rain and then half of them had been beaten back by the high surf or staved-in on the rocks. Those that succeeded in landing their men on the mole had been subjected to a murderous fire. Forty guns had been trained on the mole-head all day and every house overlooking it had musketeers posted in all its windows. It was here on the mole that Nelson received his wound, a grape-shot shattering his right elbow, and was got off in the darkness and confusion to be taken back to *Theseus*. Troubridge only learned of this afterwards, for he and his men and most of three other divisions had got ashore at the cost of heavy casualties, and having spiked the six 24-pounders on the mole were making for the rendezvous in Santa Cruz market-place. The darkness and the intricacies of a strange port defeated their purpose and they were rounded-up detachment by detachment and made prisoner by the Spanish soldiers. And the end of it, at 9 o'clock next morning, was a flag-of-truce sent by the Governor of the Canary Islands offering generous terms: all prisoners and wounded would be allowed to return to their ships on condition that the ships removed themselves from Santa Cruz Bay immediately. The terms were accepted. A hundred and fifty officers and men were killed, drowned, or missing. The cutter *Fox* had gone down, sunk by gunfire, with ninety-seven men.

"And Nelson?" demanded Hardy.

Troubridge, who had ended his story on a solemn note, brightened. "Ah now, Hardy, that's a man in a million. It was best part of an hour before the boat he was in could find *Theseus* in the wind and rain and dark, and he with his arm shattered and a dirty rag round it for a tourniquet, mark you. At last they come alongside the flagship and start shouting for a sling to be rigged, so as to get the Admiral up the side. 'Let me alone, damn you!' says he. 'I've not lost my legs, and I've still one arm!' And up the side he goes, though on a dirty night it's no child's-play even for a sound man, as you know."

Hardy nodded without enthusiasm. The stoical courage was admirable; the sacrifice of two hundred and fifty men in a totally unjustifiable assault was not. It was just what he would have expected of Horatio Nelson.

"The amputation," he began.

"They took the arm off as soon as he was aboard. Very high, near the shoulder. It's said he was sitting up dictating orders and dispatches half-an-hour after it was done."

Again the stoicism, the iron will in the frail body. Hardy could not but admire and respect it, while a carping inner voice told him that Nelson knew very well how that tale also would spread through the Fleet and add to his reputation.

"It wasn't a good amputation. He was suffering great pain when he sailed for England. As he took leave of Captain Hallowell and myself he said—" Troubridge's voice trembled slightly—"he was taking home the remains of his carcase and would be seen no more in these waters."

"And you think he means that, sir?"

"I don't know. Much, I think, depends on how the wound heals. If he doesn't return it will be a very great loss to the service."

"And if he does," Hardy said bluntly, "it would be better for the service if some other officer were given command of operations against Spanish islands."

Troubridge stiffened and his brown eyes flashed angrily.

"I believe I've a much longer acquaintance with Sir Horatio than you have, Mr Hardy," he said haughtily. "In my opinion, and not mine alone, there's no living man better fitted to command a British fleet against the enemy."

"That may well be so, sir. I beg your pardon if I appeared over-critical."

Troubridge, his sudden frown fading, seemed about to say something but finished his glass of Madeira instead.

"You'll take another glass, Captain Hardy? No?" He rose to his feet. "Then we had better go our respective ways. I hear the Nore mutiny has fizzled out," he added as they mounted to the deck, "and you'll find Lord St Vincent has stamped out the sparks among our ships off Cadiz."

"A very good thing, sir."

"Yes." They halted by the quarterdeck rail; Troubridge laid a hand on his companion's sleeve. "You know, Hardy," he said earnestly, "a man will work and fight ten times better from love than he will from fear. If there'd been a Nelson in command of every ship there'd have been no mutinies." He smiled suddenly. "You may find those propositions worth considering."

They exchanged salutes and Hardy climbed down to his waiting boat. As he was pulled across the dancing blue water to *Mutine* he reflected with some impatience that Troubridge, a capable and sensible sea-officer, appeared to be afflicted with the same purblindness as Ben Hallowell, another of Nelson's old friends. For them the little man's fine qualities quite obscured his more dubious ones; they seemed not to discern the bravado behind his undoubted bravery, the headstrong stubbornness behind his front of heroic resolution. Hardy knew, for he had experienced it himself, that Horatio Nelson could exercise a curious attraction over his fellow-men, or some of them, and that he possessed that rare and nameless power that makes a leader of men. Such attributes, in Hardy's view, could not safely be owned by an opinionated hothead who had launched that utterly hopeless frontal attack at Santa Cruz. Even Troubridge, biased as he was, could not but see the inexcusable imprudence of the second landing. If Orde or some other junior admiral not in favour with Lord St Vincent had done as much his career would have been finished, whether he lost an arm or not, he told himself irritably. And yet, when *Mutine* was running southward that afternoon and he had leisure to think of the matter again, he found himself unable to maintain this censorious posture in the face of the figure that presented itself to his mind: a skinny undersized figure

77

with a thin face pale and deeply grooved, lacking the sight of one eye and now deprived of an arm.

Mutine rejoined the Mediterranean Fleet and having made her negative report was ordered to provision, water, and await further instructions. A mail from England brought a letter from Miss Susan Manfield in a round schoolgirlish hand hoping that dear Tom was well and reminding him that it was ten months since they had said goodbye at Portsmouth. When would she see him again? She longed greatly for that time to come, and was his most affectionately with a cross to mark where she had kissed her letter. Hardy considered at some length before penning his reply. That possible promotion to post-captain could make his pay as much as ten shillings a day if he got the frigate command he coveted, but he was not the man to count chickens that were still in the egg. A safer prospect was the prize-money that would be his when the three prizes he had taken were sold. As *Mutine*'s commander his share of the proceeds would be three-eighths, and at a rough estimate—and allowing for the depredations of agents and prize-court officials—he could count on between eight hundred and a thousand pounds. It would do. His letter to Susan, brief and to the point, told her that the date of his next leave in England was uncertain but that he trusted it would be within the next two years; and that "the opportunity might then be taken for us to be united in wedlock." This letter was not marked with a cross.

The autumn and winter of 1797 was singularly uneventful for the Mediterranean Fleet. The war seemed to have shifted its focal point northward, where the long threat of the Batavian Republic's attack and invasion was at last ended by Admiral Duncan's great victory of Camperdown. Hardy, thanking his stars that he was not in a line-of-battle ship, had all the employment he wanted, for if *Mutine* was not out on patrol she was carrying St Vincent's orders and dispatches to the squadrons on blockade duty. News from home and news of what was happening in Europe came slowly and at long intervals. General Bonaparte had made the Jacobin rulers of France masters of all Italy and was invading Austria. Mr Pitt proposed to tax the wealthy classes according to the horses and carriages they possessed and the number of windows in their houses. The Government had sent an envoy to Paris with peace proposals. This last item of news sent a surge of anger through the Fleet that was only quieted when it was declared a false rumour; though those naval officers who were in touch with the political scene considered its truth more than likely. March of 1798 brought disturbing accounts of preparations to defend England from invasion across the Channel, and a copy of *The Gentleman's Magazine* that came to Hardy's notice contained diagrams of armoured rafts propelled by windmills, which (it was claimed) the French were building.

Then, in April, a frigate reached the Fleet with dispatches from England that set every vessel from the flagship to the smallest cutter in a stir of excitement and activity. The reason for the French armament that had been collecting in the Mediterranean ports was now revealed: General Bonaparte had been ordered to embark a considerable army, though it was not known whither this expedition was bound. In May Rear-Admiral Sir Horatio Nelson, with his flag hoisted in *Vanguard*, 74, was back in the Mediterranean.

2

The noonday heat of Naples at the height of midsummer enveloped Captain Troubridge and Commander Hardy as they emerged, between bowing flunkeys, from the enormous doors of the Palazzo Sessa, residence of the British Ambassador to the Court of the Two Sicilies. Both men mopped the sweat from their brows before settling their cocked hats in position and starting down the flight of marble steps.

"I'd give a hundred guineas for a fresh gale off the Forelands," Troubridge said.

Hardy grunted. "Better out here than in that furnace of a room."

At the foot of the steps on the lava-paved drive their carriage waited, its gaudily-dressed coachman flicking the flies from his horse's ears. Beyond it the Embassy gardens, cypress and azalea diversified with groups of statuary, sloped away towards the blue-silken waters of the Bay and the slowly moving sails of fishing-boats. Troubridge was about to get into the carriage when a woman stepped from behind a flowering bush close at hand and came towards them. She wore a white gown that clung to the curves of a very full figure and a wide-brimmed straw hat with coloured ribbons was perched on top of a mass of auburn curls. Troubridge doffed his hat and bowed as she approached and Hardy did the same.

"Captain Troubridge?" She looked from one to the other. "Captain Hardy?"

"Commander, ma'am," said Hardy gruffly. "His Majesty's brig-sloop *Mutine*."

Two large dark-blue eyes scrutinised him intently for a breathing-space. They were set in a face that was well-shaped though too plump for beauty. Ten years ago, he thought, she must have been a very attractive girl; then she smiled at him and he realised that the attractiveness was still there.

"You're friends of Nelson's or he wouldn't have sent you on this mission." She had a musical voice, controlled and slightly husky. "I am Emma Hamilton—he'll have spoken of me to you, I fancy."

"Sir Horatio—" Troubridge emphasised the name—"has told us of your interest with the Queen, my lady."

She nodded impatiently. "Yes. I try constantly, through Caroline, to influence Ferdinand to take the side of my country against the French. But why did he—I mean Nelson—send you instead of coming himself?"

80

Troubridge began to explain that international law required the Rear-Admiral and his squadron to remain outside neutral waters. Hardy, meanwhile, recollected what little he had learned about the politics of the Kingdom of the Two Sicilies. King Ferdinand, who it appeared cared for nothing but sport and good living, wished to preserve the neutrality which so far had been respected by the conquering French armies. Queen Caroline was the sister of the guillotined Marie Antoinette and was therefore urging her husband to launch what armed forces he possessed against Revolutionary France, in which she was supported by the ageing British Ambassador Sir William Hamilton and his wife. In spite of her doubtful antecedents Emma Hamilton had become the Queen's closest friend, and (according to Nelson) "worked night and day in the cause of England." The Neapolitan commonalty, a feudal peasantry more severely oppressed than any in Europe, were sympathetic towards the Republicans. It was, in Hardy's opinion, an odd mix-up.

"Well, never mind that," Lady Hamilton interrupted Troubridge. "I can guess what he wants—news of the French fleet, and some frigates to send in search of it. He's always short of frigates." She laughed. "I know the Navy's deepest secrets, you see."

"Just so, my lady," said Troubridge drily. "There was also the matter of an order from the King enabling the Fleet to use Sicilian ports for supplies and watering. We must have such bases if we're to scour the eastern Mediterranean for the French—"

"Egypt, or even India!" she broke in with an excitement that Hardy thought exaggerated. "That's what Nelson thinks, isn't it?" Suddenly she was pensive, finger on lip, a somewhat full-blown nymph in meditation. "It could be—yes, it could be so. This General Bonaparte has ambitions. What news Naples has of the French you know already. Thirteen of the line, nine frigates, and two hundred or more transports, all sailing eastward—our fishing-boats reported that a fortnight ago. Bonaparte's taking a great army somewhere, and it must be for a conquest larger than Malta. Tell Nelson I said he was to go to Egypt," she added imperiously to Hardy.

"Er—yes, my lady," said Hardy, with an uneasy glance at his senior; ladies of opulent charm who interested themselves in naval strategy were outside his experience.

"But I didn't wait for you in order to make guesses," she went on. "I want to know what happened at your meeting with the King. Did you get your order and your frigates?"

Troubridge hesitated, biting his lip. "I don't know that I should—"

"Oh, don't be so stupid, Captain Troubridge! Sir William—" she pronounced the name *Willum*— "was there, wasn't he? And he tells me everything. Who else was there?"

"His Majesty had with him his Secretary of State, the Marquis de Gallo," said Troubridge stiffly.

"That slimy sodomite!" spat Lady Hamilon with unexpected coarseness. "He saw to it that you got no frigates, I'll wager."

"The King deferred his decision on that point, my lady. But he directed General Acton to sign an order, on his behalf, requiring all port governors of the Two Sicilies to render assistance to the Fleet."

The Ambassador's lady laughed shortly. "That's just what Ferdinand would do. An order without the King's hand and seal at the bottom of it can be obeyed or not, as the governors feel inclined. I do believe Nelson's a better diplomatist than you, Troubridge, simple as he is."

The captain flushed. "I would not contest your ladyship's opinion. And now, if your ladyship will excuse us—"

"One moment more, sir." She changed in an instant from scorn to supplication. "I lay in wait for you to learn the result of your mission so that I might send a message, by you, to Nelson. I had to know first how you had prospered. You'll do this for me?"

"Yes, my lady," said Troubridge curtly.

Lady Hamilton turned her melting blue gaze on his companion.

"I believe I'll ask Hardy to deliver it," she murmured. "Mr Hardy—pray assure him I don't spare my labours here in his interests and those of our dear country. Tell him I'll do my best to have that port order amended. And tell him that when he returns victorious from his quest the port of Naples shall be open to his ships—and a loving welcome awaiting him."

There were undeniable tears in her lovely eyes and her very considerable bosom heaved beneath the white gown.

"Very good, ma'am—my lady," said Hardy, embarrassed.

"And—and pray, pray look after him."

On this last faltering request she turned, pressing a handkerchief to her eyes, and ran from them to vanish behind the flowering bush.

"On board with you, Hardy," snapped Troubridge; and to the Neapolitan driver, "Mola Figlio. *Mutine*'s boat. *Presto!*"

The ensuing breakneck descent of stinking alleys to the quays bereft Hardy of speech but seemed to relieve Troubridge of some ill temper. Not until they were seated in the sternsheets of the brig's boat and being pulled out to her was any comment made on what had just passed.

"Thank God we're away from the damned place," Troubridge said then. "The stink's enough to sicken a man. And the scent on that fellow De Gallo was worse."

"A slimy sodomite," Hardy repeated solemnly.

"The Frogs would call that *le mot juste*. What did you make of her, Hardy?"

"To be honest, she scared me. Half-a-dozen women in one, a different sort every minute."

"She was Sir William's kept woman before he married her," reflected Troubridge, "and Charles Greville's before that. It's not my idea of naval procedure to have a woman of that kind amending orders and opening ports for us. The Admiral—" He checked himself; the seaman rowing stroke was well within earshot. "There's an acquaintance of ours values her influence at the Neapolitan court."

"It seemed to me that she had a sort of kindness for that same acquaintance," said Hardy cautiously.

Troubridge's quick frown was transitory. "Devil a bit of it. That's the way she is—acting every moment, everything twice as large as life." He chuckled. "Another year or two and that'll apply to some other things my lady has about her."

The swarm of gaily-painted boats that had gathered round *Mutine* was being dispersed by Lieutenant Gage's strenuous shouts. Troubridge and Hardy climbed over onto her flush after-deck, the boat was hoisted inboard, and with her clewed-up sails unfurled she slowly gathered way before a light quartering wind. Naples, insubstantial as a vision, floated between sea and sky beyond the spreading furrows of the brig's wake, the mediaeval squalor of its long waterfront equated in beauty with the palaces above by the dissembling haze of the Mediterranean afternoon.

"A sink of iniquity," said Troubridge as they stood at the rail looking aft. "No other term for the place. All intriguers and double-dealers from the king to the lousiest beggar. They say you can travel from one end of it to the other by secret passages—one of 'em goes from the royal palace to the quays, at least so I've been told."

"Pity they don't convert their passages into sewers, then."

"And that's the true word, for sure. An ugly hole of a place."

"It looks a deal better from here," said Hardy.

Troubridge snorted. "Wherever I look at it from," he said, "I see danger there, Hardy."

He went below. Hardy gave an eye to the brig's canvas and a word to the helmsman and began his to-and-fro walk on the space he had designated as *Mutine*'s quarterdeck, between the mizen-mast and the after-rail. He found himself shrinking from the approaching encounter with his Rear-Admiral and was puzzled to account for it. Perhaps it was remembrance of their meeting three weeks ago, the first time he had seen Nelson for eleven months.

That meeting had shocked Hardy more than he would have admitted. It was not so much the sight of the empty right sleeve pinned to the lapel of the uniform coat as the accentuation of all the odd points about him; the face more angular and more deeply grooved, the blind eye more fixed and obvious, the untidy shock of hair now almost perfectly white, the meagre frame apparently shrunken still smaller. At a first glance he looked far older than his thirty-nine years; it was only when a smile lit the worn face and its one brilliant eye that he suddenly looked far younger. And Nelson had little to smile about just now, as Hardy knew well. He had been sent with only three ships and some frigates to discover what was going on in Toulon, and a violent storm had scattered his little squadron, dismasting and nearly wrecking his flagship. By the time hasty repairs had been made and the squadron collected again the mysterious Expedition had sailed from Toulon, no one knew whither. That the senior admirals who had been passed over in his appointment should blame him for the escape of the French was only to be expected; but to Nelson, with his craving for approbation and affection, the carping censure was like a festering wound. Now St Vincent had given him a fleet, fourteen 74's, with *Mutine* to do duty for the absent frigates he so greatly needed, to pursue the French and destroy them when he found them. *If* he found them, amended Hardy as he paced up and down. The vast French armament had a very long start, and except that it was heading eastward there had so far been no news of it. Nelson had to find them—he had to fight them and beat them soundly, too. If he failed, General Bonaparte's secret mission would triumph and the personal reputation Nelson cherished so fiercely would not be worth a button. It was doubtless the past weeks of worry and anxiety that had so aged the little Admiral, Hardy thought. And he wondered, frowning, which of those two results of failure loomed largest in Nelson's mind.

"Flagship's signalling, sir."

Midshipman Danby was steadying his glass with an arm hooked round the mizen shrouds. The line of big ships on the horizon, whose topmasts had just been visible from Naples, were now hull-up.

"Two—captains—to come aboard, sir," Danby read.

"My compliments to Captain Troubridge, Mr Danby, and the jolly-boat will be outboard in twenty minutes."

Mutine had picked up a livelier wind now that she was out in the wider bay and showed her paces before bringing-to a musket-shot away from *Vanguard*'s towering side. When Troubridge and Hardy climbed up from the jolly-boat and stepped onto the quarterdeck Nelson was waiting for them with Captain Berry and Galwey the first lieutenant. The Admiral came forward eagerly and with no pretence at dignity, his hat (as usual it was far too big for him) untidily askew on his bleached hair. Hardy found time to reflect that in any other officer this disregard for appearances would have offended his sense of naval propriety; with Nelson it stirred the kind of sympathy a man feels for the awkwardness of a child.

"Well, Troubridge—well?" Nelson demanded.

"Well only in part, Sir Horatio, I'm afraid." Troubridge produced the package he had brought with him. "The order for the Sicilian ports is here, but—"

He went on to describe the interview with King Ferdinand and his Secretary of State. All the time he was speaking the Admiral was in nervous, jerky movement, shifting his buckled shoes on the deck planking and twitching with the fingers of his left hand at the Star of the Bath on his coat-breast.

"You see, Berry?" he cried impetuously when Troubridge

had finished. "They're afraid to lend me frigates—afraid lest the French should beat me and guillotine them for assisting the British."

Berry, slim and handsome, smiled and shook his head. "They little know you, Sir Horatio."

"Indeed they do not. Well, I'll show 'em, Berry, I'll show 'em." Nelson turned quickly to Troubridge, checked something he was about to say, and then spoke with a slight hesitancy. "You saw—Lady Hamilton, perhaps?"

"We did, Sir Horatio. She charged Commander Hardy with certain messages for you personally." Troubridge paused. "She was—um—insistent that he deliver them himself."

Nelson chuckled. In a matter of seconds his face had lost its drawn and anxious look and wore a pleased smile.

"Her ladyship has a way of getting what she wants—and that, gentlemen, is a most fortunate circumstance for our country. Well, Hardy—the messages?"

Hardy gulped, in some embarrassment. He had Emma Hamilton's words clear in his mind but found difficulty in starting his report. There were the beginnings of a frown on the Admiral's brow by the time he began to speak.

"Lady Hamilton first instructed me to tell you that you must go to Egypt, Sir Horatio—"

"She thinks as I do!" Nelson interrupted delightedly, glancing from Berry to Troubridge. "General Bonaparte—but go on, Hardy, go on."

"I was to assure you that she doesn't spare her labours in your interests, Sir Horatio, and those of England. And that she would do her best to have the port order amended. And—" Hardy's deep voice, already formal, became perfectly expressionless. "And that when you return victorious the port of Naples will be open to the Fleet and a—a loving welcome awaiting yourself."

The Admiral's mouth had fallen slightly open at the last sentence. Now he turned away and wiped his sleeve across his eyes. In a moment, however, he had swung round, his odd face shining and his head thrown back.

"And I swear by high heaven," he cried, "that I'll return victorious or not at all!"

It was almost ludicrously theatrical and yet (Hardy felt sure) it was not intended for effect; at least, not for effect on those who stood round him. Was it, perhaps, that Nelson acted for an audience of one—himself? But now the extraordinary man was once again the plain sea-officer, his features settled and stern and his good eye cocked aloft to observe the wind.

"A fair breeze, gentlemen," he said briskly. "We'll waste not a moment more. Troubridge—Hardy—you'll forgive my not asking you below to my cabin. Captain Berry, I'll trouble you to make to the Fleet 'Prepare to make sail.' Captain Troubridge, *Mutine*'s boat will put you aboard *Culloden*."

He laid his hand on Hardy's sleeve as they went to the rail.

"*Mutine* is all the frigates I have and you'll be worked hard," he said. "But I promise you a real frigate the instant I can find one for you."

"Thankee, Sir Horatio," said Hardy.

Mutine was indeed worked hard. Her inquisitive bows went prying into the bays and harbours, ports and inlets, of the eastern Mediterranean without a day's cessation for the next six weeks, and except for the few hours she spent at anchor in Syracuse harbour to take in water and provisions she was virtually the whole time under sail. So far from grudging this continual service, Hardy was well content with it. He had long ago moulded Gage into the sort of first lieutenant he wanted and established his precepts of strict order and instant obedience among his crew, and he knew that Nelson could not use his 74's as frigates. With a French fleet of thirteen of the line and nine frigates at sea somewhere in the Mediterranean, the Admiral had to hold his own ships together in readiness for battle; he had in fact already formed them into three squadrons and arranged the method of attack should the French be encountered at sea, and as time passed and it became increasingly probable that they had reached an anchorage his plan for attacking an enemy fleet at anchor was hammered out at the councils-of-war on board *Vanguard*. There was ample opportunity for some or all of the captains to attend Nelson's councils and dinners aboard the flagship, for the Fleet's progress was necessarily slow and the big ships frequently lay hove-to until such time as *Mutine* came back to report on her latest landward excursion.

The news that Malta had fallen to the French, who had left a garrison there and sailed on, came from a Ragusan brig intercepted by *Mutine*. It had sent Nelson on a direct course for Alexandria as fast as his ships could sail. His presentiment (and Lady Hamilton's) that Bonaparte's goal was Egypt seemed confirmed, for the steady westerly wind was foul for Sicily, the likeliest alternative, and fair for the Egyptian port. When *Mutine* had returned from looking into the port, where she had found no French ships, the Admiral's disappointment threw him into a depression that came near to being an illness. Not until many days later was it revealed that he had been too quick; the French, delaying at Malta and steering a course well to the south of Nelson's, were in fact behind him. He had missed them by a single day.

On went the hunters then, north to the Turkish Gulf of Antalya, east to the Pelopponese, back again to Syracuse after a month of searching. Syracuse alone of the Sicilian ports semed to have received Lady Hamilton's promised 'amendment' to King Ferdinand's order, and the Fleet provisioned and watered there. And here a captured Spanish wine-brig provided the news that the French armament had been seen four weeks ago steering to the south-east from Candia. It was now practically certain that Nelson had been ahead of them and that their goal was indeed Egypt. Once more the fourteen ships sailed for Alexandria; and this time the passage took them only four days. On the first day of August *Swiftsure* and *Alexander* were detached, with *Mutine*, to look into the port, and for the second time the British hopes were dashed. There were no French ships at Alexandria.

Hardy heard afterwards from Troubridge how Nelson, in despair, had cried out that his heart was broken. But that terrible fit of depression was to last a few hours only. The Fleet had turned eastward along the Egyptian coast with *Goliath* and *Zealous* leading, and a little before four o'clock in the afternoon *Zealous* was observed to be signalling the flagship. A signal midshipman dashed down to the cabin where Nelson and some of his captains were ending a silent meal. *Enemy in sight. Ships moored in line of battle in Aboukir Bay.* There was a spontaneous cheer as the signal was read out, and then Nelson rose from the table with a face (said Troubridge) blazing with joy. "Gentlemen," he told them, "by this time tomorrow I shall have gained a peerage or Westminster Abbey."

3

The commander of the *Mutine* was sitting a trifle uncomfortably at the foremasthead of his ship, with his left arm hooked round the mast and his heels resting on the wind-filled canvas of the foretopsail below him. The brig's topgallants and royals were clewed-up and she was swooping lightly over the swell in Aboukir Bay under topsails, outer jib, and driver, so that Hardy had a clear view all round him. The glorious hues of early evening in the Mediterranean had taken the place of the afternoon glare, and the sails of the ten great ships on the brig's starboard beam shone pale gold as they moved in to attack, their apparent confusion in marked contrast with the orderly line of French ships lying at anchor a mile ahead. Using his glass, Hardy counted thirteen enemy ships; the very large Frenchman in the centre of the motionless line would be the flagship *L'Orient*, 120 guns. Nearer at hand, marking the northern horn of the long bay the British were entering, he could see a small rocky islet with a fort or battery on it —Aboukir Island. There was shoal water all round that island, he knew, and it was more than likely that the whole bay was shallow.

Hardy shifted his massive rump on the hard round of the yard, feeling the lift and 'scend of the brig over the rolling swell. It was hardly proper for a captain to post himself at the masthead in such circumstances, but he could not bring himself to forgo the opportunity of witnessing the beginning of the action. The little *Mutine* could not take part in the battle of giants; it would be some time before there was any task for her. Meanwhile, he could observe the Admiral's plan of attack in actual operation.

Looking astern through the rigging of the upper spars on main and mizen, he could see the remaining four ships of the British fleet. One of them, the 50-gun *Leander*, was sailing on the quarter of the rearmost 74; with little more gun-power than a frigate, her rôle was a subordinate one. The other three were a long way astern, under all the sail they could wear but still advancing very slowly before the light and fitful northeasterly breeze. *Swiftsure* and *Alexander* had been delayed by their scouting activities off Alexandria and *Culloden* had been detached earlier to take in tow a captured French store-ship. Hardy could imagine Troubridge's wild impatience. However, the battle could hardly end before *Culloden* came up, and Troubridge would have his part in a victory greater than that of St Vincent eighteen months ago. He caught himself up on that thought. Victory? Here was the impetuous Nelson heading into shoal waters without any reliable chart, attacking with ten ships instead of waiting for his full strength, to fight an action a great part of which would be in darkness—and he, Hardy, had assumed without hesitation that the French would be utterly defeated. Had he at last been converted to Troubridge's faith?

Three nights ago, when he had dined on board *Culloden* by invitation of her captain, Troubridge had laboured to persuade him that a man might be a great genius in one direction though he was a simpleton in others; that Horatio Nelson, for all his oddities and failings, knew better than any other man alive how to defeat the French at sea. He had described those frequent councils at which every possible aspect of attack had been discussed and fully planned, and how they had impressed the captains who were present at them. Foley, Hallowell, Saumarez, Louis, Ball, Hood—Hardy knew and respected them for experienced sea-officers and could not ignore their opinion. That they all, like Troubridge, were ready to follow Nelson wherever he led was the mark of their faith, and though they might be swayed by that curiously attractive personality of his it could not possibly be a blind faith. Nelson, said Troubridge, had called them his "band of brothers". (Against his will Hardy had found himself envious.) But this certainty of present victory, reflected the big man at the masthead, came chiefly from the brilliant simplicity of Nelson's plan of attack, as Troubridge had reported it.

He returned his attention to the ships ahead. The leading 74's were hauling to the wind to weather the shoals off Aboukir Island. He watched anxiously as the rest followed; these big unbroken rollers surging towards the distant shore were a sure sign of a very gradual shoaling, and another sign was that the French line was anchored a long way out from the coast. The French admiral (De Brueys, it was rumoured) would of course have anchored his line as close in to the shallows as possible, so that it could not be attacked from that side. His ships were all bows-on to the northerly wind and their starboard broadsides would be ready and waiting while the guns on the landward side would be unprepared. For the form of attack De Brueys would confidently anticipate was the accepted line-of-battle procedure: each enemy ship coming board-and-board with an opponent and both of them battering away until one or other hauled down her colours. And with his superior gun-power he had then a chance at least of victory.

Hardy remembered Troubridge's elation as he had described Nelson's unorthodox plan—a plan which, as he pointed out, actually turned the enemy's strength into weakness. It was based on two obvious facts: first, that moored against the shoals as they were no enemy ships could manoeuvre, and—second —that an anchored ship must have room to swing, which meant room for another ship to pass between her and the shoal. The British fleet would therefore concentrate on the French van from the flagship to the northern end of the line, and every ship of the van would be attacked from both sides. The rear ships could be dealt with later. "And I'll tell you this, Hardy," Troubridge had ended his account, "he won't be happy unless he takes or destroys the lot of 'em."

There was no grudging in Hardy's approval this time. He knew he could not have thought of such a plan himself and he was certain it could not be bettered. He spared a thought for General Bonaparte and his great army, doubtless landed weeks ago, marooned in the deserts with no hope of supplies or reinforcements, incapable of proceeding. Undoubtedly this would be a world-shaking victory—and to Horatio Nelson it would bring the fame and adulation for which he craved so persistently.

The sun was a red ball just above the purple-brown haze of the horizon. On the deck ninety feet below him a seaman ran for'ard to strike four bells of the first dog-watch. A glance astern showed him *Culloden* with her spread of sail crimson in the sunset, still two miles or more away but ahead of *Swiftsure* and *Alexander*, making the best of the light breeze and rolling considerably in the cross-swell that was running into the bay. And now, a mile ahead, two British ships were closing-in to the French line—*Goliath* and *Zealous*, racing to be first through. There went the first shots, the leading Frenchman opening fire as *Goliath* crossed her bows, the reports merging with the ragged explosion of *Goliath*'s raking broadside. Hardy's glass was at his eye to mark *Zealous*, in a girdle of smoke and yellow flame, passing between the next two ships. *Orion*—*Theseus*—*Audacious*—"By God!" he said aloud. "Five of ours between shoal and line!" The plan was in operation before his eyes. Nelson's *Vanguard* was the first ship to take the seaward side, and the thunder of her engagement drummed in his ears. He noted two others—*Minotaur* and *Defence*, he thought—passing her followed by *Bellerophon*, who went on to anchor board-and-board with *Orient* in the centre of the line. A 74 challenged a 120-gun ship and the shock of their encounter seemed to shake the mast at his side.

But now the sun was down and the swift twilight falling. Hardy became aware that the myriad flashes of the guns were brighter than the last of the daylight, and that the great banks of smoke rolling up to the clear green of the sky overhead were veiling from him any further details of the fight. With the unceasing roar of the guns in his ears he slid down to the deck and went aft.

"All guns loaded, sir, crews standing by," said Gage, a thin silhouette against the pale glimmer of sea and sky.

"Very well, Mr Gage. Don't run out, and keep the ports closed. Send a good man to the masthead, if you please." Hardy turned to the quartermaster. "Starboard a point, Collins. Hold her so."

Mutine crept closer in to the inferno of noise and flame. It was impossible to gauge the progress of the battle; at the southern end of the great bank of flame-shot smoke it was clear enough to see the dim shapes, bare-poled and motionless, of the French rear ships. Hardy had the brig hove-to when she was two cable-lengths from the edge of the smoke-cloud, and was waiting, alert for any chance of service or action, when the masthead lookout hailed the deck.

"Cap'n, sir! Looks as if one of ourn's gorn aground. Astern, sir, orf the island."

Hardy sprang into the shrouds and gazed northward. The sky in this quarter was clear of smoke and already ablink with stars. A flash a mile or so away, low down on the water, apprised him that the battery on Aboukir Island was firing at something, and well to the right of it he made out the shape of a big ship, seemingly motionless. Farther still to the right two other dark shapes, slightly more distant than the first and each with a twinkle of lanterns at the masthead, moved across the humped waves. Hardy made his deduction instantly. *Culloden* had been ahead, and it was she who had struck on the shoal; no doubt Troubridge had cut the corner too sharply in his impatience. The grounded ship had served as a beacon for the two ships astern of her, and *Alexander* and *Swiftsure*, displaying the night signal ordered by the Admiral, were giving the shoal a wide berth.

"Hands to make sail!"

Black figures spidered aloft and *Mutine*'s upper sails bellied out from the yards. The brig paid off on the larboard tack, reaching eastward close-hauled with the pandemonium of the battle raging in the smoky blackness astern. An inarticulate but urgent hail from the masthead made Hardy suddenly aware of the hulk drifting before the wind on *Mutine*'s starboard bow little more than a musket-shot away. He saw that it was a 74, totally dismasted except for a stump of foremast on which a rag of sail had been rigged. She was near enough to hail, and her name came wailing back on the night wind.

"*Bellerophon!*"

"Can I give you any help?"

"Nothing you can do!" answered the passing voice.

She drifted on into the darkness as the brig went about on the starboard tack. So *Orient*'s 60-gun broadside had accounted for one British 74. Hardy stared at the enigmatic thundercloud of the battle, now on the larboard quarter, and wondered for a moment how *Vanguard* was faring. He had changed his mind about Nelson's capacity as an admiral but not about his prudence; that was non-existent. The man still needed looking after. Hardy shook himself irritably and snapped at the helmsman.

"Steer small, can't you! Meet her on this swell!"

The wind had freshened and the swell rolling across the bay had increased. As *Mutine* neared the black bulk of the *Culloden* a heavy thud accompanied by a medley of creaks, cracks, and groans could be distinctly heard at intervals; she was lifting and pounding on the shoal. Now and again there came the report of a gun from the battery on Aboukir Island, but from the sound Hardy judged it was only a 12-pounder and likely enough out of range. The brig's light draught would have enabled her to sail completely round the stranded 74, but the heavy swell prevented her from sheering alongside. Hardy brought her as close as he dared and hailed in a voice that rose above the periodic thud and grind and the flapping of loose canvas. It was Troubridge's voice that came faintly across the gap of heaving water.

"Hardy? Here's a damned mess . . . pounding her heart out . . . of all the born bloody fools I'm the damnedest."

"We'll try to tow you off!" Hardy bellowed.

"There's a chance—yes." The words came intermittently, punctuated by the noises of sea and ship. "Tip of shoal . . . holding her . . . haul bows round. My boat . . . line."

Rightly interpreting this as meaning that *Culloden* would send a boat with a line, and that the aim would be to tow so that the ship's bows were brought to starboard, Hardy set about preparing the brig for her task. And so began a Herculean labour that was to last for seven hours, while a mile or two to the southward the British fleet fought the most important battle of the century without the aid of the unhappy *Culloden*.

Clouds veiled the stars. The angry red stars of gunfire in the black smoke-pyre to southward, whence came the ceaseless uproar of the fight, took their place. Through the pitchy dark of the Egyptian night the combined crews of the brig and the 74, more than 800 men, strove and failed and strove again. It was during the second attempt to tow *Culloden* off, at about four bells of the first watch, that the distant battle-smoke became irradiated with a mounting crimson glow. Half-an-hour later a vast explosion, stunning even in the ears of the toilers on the Aboukir shoal, drew the gaze of every man to the gigantic flame that towered above the smoke and hung there in terrible glory for many minutes. The detonation seemed to arrest the fighting, for a curious silence succeeded it. Then the clamour of the guns burst out again with redoubled fury. This, as Hardy learned next day, was the blowing-up of *Orient* with 1,200 men on board.

Culloden's timbers were being weakened by the incessant pounding on the shoal and by midnight the clanking of her pumps was continuous. Her foretopmast came down with a splintering crack while the final vain attempt to tow her off was being made. To kedge her off with anchors laid out and cables led to the capstans was the next step to be taken; main and mizen topgallant masts snapped while this was being tried. Hardy, drenched to the skin from his work in charge of one of *Mutine*'s boats, felt rather than saw the faint lightening of the darkness and the first pale glimmer of dawn. From *Culloden*'s lurching deck came Troubridge's voice, hoarse with shouting, urging on the men straining at the capstan bars. They were still straining at the bars, with no effect, when dawn spread into growing daylight and the gunfire in the south dwindled and ceased.

Out of the paling greyness, through the last murky wreaths of gunsmoke, the shapes of great ships swam into the circle of Hardy's glass. He identified *Vanguard* first, her topsails in shreds but every mast standing. Two other 74's had been less fortunate, for both had lost maintopmasts. But the confused mass of shipping, two dozen huge hulls floating on a sea almost solid with broken spars and planks and other debris, answered instantly the eager question in his mind, for every vessel was wearing British colours.

A ship smaller than the rest had hoisted sail and was making towards *Mutine* and *Culloden*. She was the 50-gun *Leander*, and she appeared to have suffered but little in the battle though judging by the holes in her sails she had taken some part in it. Troubridge, seeing her, set his weary men to work fothering *Culloden*'s damaged bottom with oakum and canvas; the brig and the fourth-rate between them would exert sufficient force to pull his ship's bows from the shoal. *Leander* hove-to abeam of *Mutine* and lowered a boat, but Thomson, her captain, was shouting from his quarterdeck before the boat touched the water.

"A great victory, Hardy! Nine taken, two burnt. Only two of 'em got away."

"Is the Admiral unhurt?"

"Wounded in the head," Thomson replied; and Hardy felt a stab of anxiety. "Not serious, though—he's up and at it as usual, writing Fleet orders as fast as his pen'll go. One of 'em's coming over to you in my boat."

Hardy read the Fleet order a few minutes later: *"Almighty God having blessed His Majesty's arms with victory, the admiral intends returning public thanksgiving for the same at two o'clock today, and he recommends every ship doing the same as soon as convenient."*

4

It was nearing sunset when *Mutine*'s jolly-boat pulled towards the flagship, but the smell of burnt powder and charred timber still hung on the air. Hardy, in the sternsheets, looked round him at a throng of ruined ships, some of them, like *Conquérant* and *Guerrier*, with ragged gaps in their sides through which a coach and four could have driven, others with their masts reduced to splintered stumps. From every ship, whether victor or prize, came the sound of many hammers at work. But it would be a month at least, thought Hardy, before Aboukir Bay would see the last of these battered hulks. The reward of victory for the 7,000 British seamen who had survived the Battle of the Nile would be weeks of hard and unremitting toil.

He had learned already that the Fleet's losses were estimated to be 200 killed and 700 wounded. Of the French, more than 5,000 were thought to have been killed or drowned. Two hundred French prisoners were being kept to help with the work of repair, and the rest—3,000 men—were to be sent under cartel to the French commandant at Aboukir. All this, with its concomitants of transport arrangements, food, surgery and the rest, had to be planned and organised; reports from all ships collated; orders of all kinds issued; dispatches written. And for all the Admiral was responsible. He had his secretary and clerk to assist him, and no doubt his flag-captain would have to shoulder a good deal of the work, especially as Nelson had been wounded in the head. Hardy thanked his stars he was not a flag-captain. He wondered why *Vanguard* had signalled him to come on board.

The boat was nearing the flagship now, and his eye took in the many scars of battle she bore; the splintered holes in her side, the blackened timber along her double row of gunports, the missing sections of the rail above and the dangling ends of cordage overhead. Much of the chaos had been reduced to a sort of order and when he stepped onto the quarterdeck he found rows of seamen on hands and knees holystoning the deck. Most of the dark stains had been swabbed from the planking but there must have been many; according to Thomson, *Vanguard*'s casualties had been heavier than those of any other British ship except *Bellerophon*.

Captain Berry came across the deck to greet Hardy. He was

hatless, his white breeches had a red-brown stain across them, and he was unshaven. His handsome face looked grey and weary. On the few occasions when they had encountered each other before Hardy had found him curt and somewhat supercilious, but this evening he had a brief smile and a grasp of the hand for *Mutine*'s commander.

"The colonel of Marines is with him now," he said, "but you won't have to wait long. He's very anxious to see you, Hardy."

"How's his wound, sir?" Hardy asked.

Berry frowned and wagged his head. "He won't have the dressing changed. Says he hasn't time for it. It's not deep, but I fear the consequences if he insists on neglecting it. It was a piece of langridge that slit his scalp."

"Oh." Hardy's frown reflected the flag-captain's. "That won't do. We can't spare him, after this."

He heard himself say the words with some surprise.

"Indeed we can't." Berry seemed to hesitate, then spoke impulsively. "Hardy, I'm being sent home with the dispatches. If you—yes, Mr O'Neill?"

The midshipman who had approached them saluted. "The Admiral asks if Captain Hardy is on board, sir."

"Conduct Captain Hardy to Sir Horatio. And the best of good fortune go with you, Hardy."

An odd sort of valediction that, thought Hardy as he followed the midshipman below. However, Berry was taking home the dispatches, which meant a knighthood for certain, so he could afford to be extra affable. He acknowledged the salute of the marine sentry outside the day cabin and went in.

The big lamp hanging from the deckhead was already alight. Beneath it three tables had been pushed together to make a long desk. The Admiral was seated at its centre, Secretary Comyn and a clerk at the ends, and all three were scratching away busily with their quills. To Hardy's eye there seemed to be paper everywhere; and the Admiral's face, or what could be seen of it, was as white as the paper and whiter than the dingy bandage that was swathed across his head and over his right eye. Nelson glanced up as Hardy advanced to the table, and his drawn features twisted in a grim little smile.

"I'm told you have the broadest shoulders in my Fleet, Hardy," he said abruptly, "and that's as well. I am going to lay a heavy burden on them."

He looked ill with fatigue. Hardy, seeking appropriate words for his reply, felt a stabbing pang of compassion.

"If it'll take any weight off yours, Sir Horatio," he said with more feeling than usual, "I'll be more than happy, whatever it is."

"Berry goes home with dispatches. I signed this at noon."

Nelson held out a paper and Hardy took it. It was his commission as post-captain. He was to be captain of *Vanguard*, Nelson's flag-captain. A fleeting vision of the frigate he had hoped to command rose before his eyes and faded.

"Thankee, Sir Horatio," said Captain Hardy.

FOUR

1

Captain Hardy commanded the *Vanguard*, 74, for ten months. At the end of them he had aged ten years, or felt he had. Looking back from the calm of veritable old age, he saw the period between August 1798 and October 1799 as a year and a quarter of nightmare; for the trouble did not end when he left *Vanguard* for *Foudroyant*. It was not, perhaps, so much like a nightmare as like one of those evil but less fantastic dreams wherein the dreamer sees catastrophe approaching and is powerless to prevent it.

His first three weeks in command were happy enough, for Hardy had never been so busy in his life. The Admiral's head wound was slow to heal, as might have been expected, and pain and an intermittent fever between them confined him to his cabin for much of the time. The responsibility for getting the battered British ships and their even more battered prizes fit for sea fell largely on the new flag-captain, and since Hardy's capability for work that he understood was inexhaustible he shouldered the burden with complete success. All the same, it was not until the evening of August 19th that *Vanguard* was able to sail from Aboukir Bay. She was not this time the flagship of a fine fleet of thirteen vessels but one of a trio of slow-sailing hulks that included *Minotaur* and *Audacious*; in such groups, sailing as best they could with jury rigs against the contrary westerlies of late summer, the victors of the Nile and their prizes began the 1,700-mile voyage to Naples Bay and the dockyards of Castellamare. Vulnerable though they were, they had nothing to fear from an enemy. Once again the British were masters of the Mediterranean.

It was on this voyage, which lasted nearly five weeks, that Captain Hardy's imperturbability and patience were most severely tried. The Admiral, recovering as soon as the flagship began to feel the sea-breezes, was on deck every day and for much of the time in his captain's company. He was in a state of perpetual restlessness, by turns moody and feverishly excited, fidgety over details and impatient with *Vanguard*'s slow progress. Hardy constrained himself to pliability with these moods but only up to a point. He had come round to the opinion of Troubridge and Berry and the rest, that Horatio Nelson was a great leader and sea-officer, and the querulous semi-invalid of this period was still Horatio Nelson; but he would not on that account abandon his right to speak his own mind and command his own ship.

"Captain Hardy, I see you have Midshipman the Honourable Radstock keeping a watch on deck."

"Yes, Sir Horatio."

"He didn't do so in Captain Berry's time."

"No, Sir Horatio? But he does so in Captain Hardy's time."

"H'm. Very well."

Discipline, in Hardy's opinion, had been allowed to become dangerously slack in *Vanguard* under her previous captain. He had wrought mightily to rectify this and he was not going to have his work undone.

"What's this, Hardy? A flogging? You know I detest the business!"

"I know it, Sir Horatio. I'm sorry myself there should have been occasion for it. Six lashes for theft—the minimum punishment, as you're aware. The case is proved beyond doubt. If the thief doesn't suffer now his messmates will suffer from him later."

The Admiral had turned away and gone below without replying. After these exchanges—and there were a hundred such—Hardy had no reason to regret his firmness; Nelson seemed to repose more rather than less confidence in him. But these, which Hardy thought of as his reasonable frettings, were far more easy for the captain to cope with than the almost hysterical outbursts of his darker moods which grew wilder as *Vanguard* drew nearer to her destination.

"Hardy! I'm going home—I shall apply for leave—my mind is fixed. I need medical attention."

"You certainly need a rest, Sir Horatio. But—"

"Lord St Vincent will promote Troubridge if I ask it. You'd be happy to serve under Troubridge, Hardy?"

"Very happy, Sir Horatio. It would—"

"I recall Troubridge once said he modelled himself on me. Well, my God, the copy's a damned deal better than the original!—I'll write to Lord St Vincent this moment."

This was during the morning watch on September 7th. Nelson came on deck again at the beginning of the first watch that same night and joined the captain in his quarterdeck walk.

"I can't give up, Hardy," he said in a piteous tone, after pacing for a long time in silence. "What would they do without me?"

Not long ago Hardy would have hidden a sneer behind his impassivity and thought to himself, *I fancy they'll manage.* Now he was not so sure that they could. He was well aware that when the news of the Nile battle became known Nelson would be the hero not only of the Navy but also of the nation, a figure symbolic of victory and essential to it.

"We all know your worth, Sir Horatio," he contented himself with saying.

"Yes, Hardy, yes—of course I must stay."

But two days later Nelson was in the dumps again and his secretary, Comyn, was hard at it drafting and re-drafting letters of resignation to Lord Spencer at the Admiralty.

Hardy found it hard to reconcile this vacillatory personage with the daring and resolute man who had sailed unhesitatingly into battle at Aboukir Bay. But his sympathy was heartfelt, undiluted now with any scorn. He sensed the little Admiral's need for understanding and affection and knew himself incapable of supplying it, or at least of expressing it.

Stromboli was in sight on the starboard bow when *Mutine*, who had taken news and dispatches to Naples, joined the flagship with *Thalia* and two other frigates. The pile of congratulatory letters (there was one, Comyn told Hardy, from Lady Hamilton) threw the Admiral into an ecstasy of delight. The furious squall that struck the little squadron two days later, snapping off *Vanguard*'s jury foremast and the head of her maintopmast, cast him into despair again. After that mishap Hardy could forget for several hours all problems of sentiment in the more congenial task of controlling a dismasted ship, holed in four places and only temporarily patched up, in a sea that boiled like a cauldron under the blast of the *gregale*. And in the end *Vanguard*, towed by *Thalia*, limped into the Bay of Naples on the morning of September 22nd.

From a stance in the maintop Captain Hardy watched the cypress-clad hills and the port below them grow out of a plain of blue water as smooth as a mirror. Through his glass as *Vanguard* crept nearer he could see the steep tiers of houses, pink and terracotta and yellow, and a swarm of boats, feluccas, and every kind of craft filling the space in front of the quays. The quays themselves were already black with people (most of them, he recalled, would be beggars or thieves) and it was not hard to foresee the sort of welcome that awaited the Victor of the Nile, the saviour of Naples from the French. Doubtless the British Ambassador—and his wife, of course—would come out to the ship, and that meant a salute of thirteen guns. If King Ferdinand brought his long nose out to her as well, that meant twenty-one guns. Hardy clambered down to the deck. The Admiral, wearing his best coat with the gold lace and embroidered star, halted his restless pacing of the quarterdeck as Hardy came up to him and touched his hat in salute.

"I submit, Sir Horatio," he said, "that *Vanguard* anchors off Castellamare and well out from the shore, to avoid being mobbed by small craft."

Nelson nodded. He no longer wore a bandage, and the angry red scar on his forehead stood out conspicuously against the pallor of his face, which wore a look of anxiety as he gazed frowningly towards distant Naples. Hardy saw his expression with some surprise; he had expected the Admiral to be highly elated.

"Mark this, Hardy," Nelson said in a low voice, still looking towards the port on the blue horizon. "I must have rest, so I shall spend four or five days here with Sir William Hamilton —not more. These times are not for idleness."

Troubridge's words spoken three months ago recurred to the flag-captain : *I see danger there, Hardy.* The Admiral's face, he thought, seemed to be saying that now.

"It's a country of fiddlers and poets, whores and scoundrels," Nelson went on, half to himself. "In future Syracuse shall be my port." He swung round to face the captain. "Hardy, I rely upon you to speed *Vanguard*'s repairs."

"Castellamare isn't Chatham, Sir Horatio," Hardy said bluntly. "She'll be in dock for more than four or five days."

"You'll do your best as always, I know."

"I will, sure."

Hardy said that emphatically, with one of his rare smiles. He was wonderfully relieved by this resolve to leave Naples at the earliest opportunity. He went off to seek Galwey, his first lieutenant, and arrange for the formalities and salutes involved in receiving an ambassador and possibly a foreign royalty on board his ship.

Two hours later *Vanguard*'s guns were thundering out the 13-gun salute, and shortly after it the 21 guns required by the King of the Two Sicilies. Scarcely had the flagship cast off her tow and dropped anchor when the British Ambassador's barge was seen approaching. Accompanying it was a larger barge crammed with musicians playing *Rule, Britannia*. The first visitor to step onto the quarterdeck was the Ambassador's wife, and Hardy, standing on one side, saw Nelson's face colour and light up as he went forward to meet her. Lady Hamilton was wearing a filmy white dress with blue ribbons fluttering from sleeves and neck, and her auburn hair was bound with a broader ribbon displaying the legend NELSON AND VICTORY. She took one or two faltering steps towards the Admiral and paused, one hand to her head and the other gracefully outstretched.

"Oh God—is it possible?" she cried, and swooned into the Admiral's one arm.

It would have been more effective but for Captain Hardy. Doubting whether so voluptuous a form could in fact be supported by an arm so thin and wasted, he took a swift pace forward and took the lady's weight on his large palms, like buffers. She recovered herself quickly, and the glance she darted at her supporter was so venomous that he lost no time in retreating into the background. From behind the red-coated rank of marines woodenly presenting arms he watched the rest of the show.

Sir William Hamilton, tall and thin and venerable in black satin; some nameless Neapolitan aristocrats in all the colours of the rainbow; showers of congratulations, shrill ecstasies, kissing of hands, deafening chatter. Here came another barge all gold from stem to stern, another boatload of blaring musicians—*See the Conquering Hero Comes*—and fat King Ferdinand sweating in powder and gold lace, attended by bejewelled courtiers whose breeches alone determined their sex. Nelson's small form was engulfed in their lavish adulation; but the white gown and ample bosom of Emma Hamilton clung close to him always.

It was soon plain that the Admiral was to be hurried away.

He went down to the ambassadorial barge looking like a man walking in his sleep, and without farewell to his flag-captain. Hardy watched the barges and their floating orchestras (still playing fortissimo) pull towards the port, accompanied by a vociferous throng of boats that had come out to meet them. He saw them near the quays, where flags and bunting hung from every building, and noted the wheeling cloud of a thousand birds liberated in honour of the conqueror. Then he snapped his glass shut and turned, his foot striking against some object that was rolling on the deck. It was a jewelled pomander on a broken ribbon; he had noticed it dangling from the wrist of one of the King's gentlemen-in-waiting.

"Mr Galwey!" he said briskly. "Clear the quarterdeck, if you please, and send half-a-dozen hands to swab it down. Then call my gig away. I'm going over to the dockyard."

2

She stepped onto the quarterdeck of the *Vanguard* as lightly as a ballet-dancer despite her bulk. It was December now and the *tramontana* was sending its icy draught from the high hills north of Vesuvius, so the half-dozen Neapolitan fashionables of both sexes who had come on board with her were shivering in furs. Emma Hamilton was wearing a fur-trimmed pelisse whose hood allowed her auburn locks to escape and dance in the cold wind. Captain Hardy had to admit that the colour in her cheeks suited well with those strikingly blue eyes. He lifted his hat and bowed stiffly. Lady Hamilton left her entourage to gather round Lieutenants Galwey and Watson, who were on deck-watch, and crossed the deck to the captain, who had not advanced to meet her. Her smile was brief and artificial.

"I'm sorry indeed, Hardy," she said without preamble, "that my message didn't reach you."

Hardy said nothing. She knew very well that he had received

her message. Emma's full lips compressed themselves a trifle before she went on.

"It's about the boat's crew who conveyed Count Vanni and the Marquis Velletri ashore four days ago. The poor fellows were tempted into a *taverna* and took too much wine."

"I'm aware of it, my lady," said Hardy drily. "They defied the midshipman in charge and deserted the boat. I had to send a lieutenant and six hands to fetch them on board."

"They knew their fault—they came and asked me to intercede for them." The blue eyes had narrowed. "I'm told they've been severely punished."

"They have been punished precisely as they deserved, my lady." The captain's tone was entirely without expression. "Twelve lashes for their crime. An extra twelve lashes for applying to your ladyship for protection."

Lady Hamilton drew in her breath with an audible hiss and her gaze was like a blue flame.

"And I've promised the same reward," he continued evenly, before she could speak, "to any man who asks a civilian to aid him in escaping justice."

For an instant he thought she was going to strike him. Then she controlled herself.

"You—you big slob!" she whispered venomously. "Be sure that Nelson shall hear of this!" She raised her voice. "Thank you, Captain Hardy, for your courtesy.—*Miei amici, andiamo.*"

She swung on her heel, collected her Neapolitan escort, and went down to the barge that had brought them out to the ship.

Hardy stood quite still for half-a-minute, his large unruffled countenance turned towards Naples. He could just hear the multitudinous murmur from the distant quays and alleys but he could only imagine (thank God) their stink. He had always disliked the place, and in the twelve weeks that had passed since *Vanguard*'s arrival after the Battle of the Nile dislike had intensified to hatred. He turned his back on Naples and went to the quarterdeck rail, to stare at the steel-blue horizon of the winter Mediterranean and recapitulate the happenings of that autumn.

The first three weeks had been Bedlam, by what Hardy had seen and heard of them. The celebrations of victory were never-ending. The scores of great villas and palaces hung out banners and illuminations, gave firework displays and balls and dinner-parties, discharged in the small hours their carriage-loads of inebriated Neapolitan nobility. The slums and tortuous alleys of the port roared with singing, fighting, and drunken revelry, and the *lazzaroni*, the great tribe of beggars and thieves whose patron was King Ferdinand himself, paraded the streets day and night and forced every merchant to strengthen his shutters and double-lock his doors. Nelson's birthday set off another train of explosive rejoicing. The Hamiltons' dinner in his honour brought eighteen hundred guests to the Palazzo Sessa, the wealthier of whom were already planning dinner-parties for Nelson at their own palaces. A new verse praising Nelson was added to the British National Anthem and sung by Lady Hamilton. More banners and illuminations, more fireworks, images of Nelson in wax and plaster, *tableaux vivants* of the hero being crowned and enwreathed by angels. The centre of it all, the Admiral who so sorely needed four or five days of rest, sat up night after night in full-dress uniform receiving the adulation of an effete aristocracy who had resolved to make an idol of him. At his side Emma Hamilton continually assured him that he deserved all this and far more besides. "And he laps it up—why wouldn't he?" said Troubridge bitterly; he and Captain Ball of the *Alexander* had been at the birthday dinner.

Troubridge and Hardy saw a great deal of each other in those days. *Vanguard* lay next to *Culloden* in the Castellamare dockyard and the two captains were moving heaven and earth—or their equivalent, the Neapolitan dockyard officials—to get their ships repaired and ready for sea. Troubridge in particular went at this task like a madman, badgering and bullying with a complete disregard for ranks and titles; the ignominious part played by *Culloden* in Aboukir Bay and the recent news of his wife's death, thought Hardy, were both at the back of this furious activity. When they met, dining amid the racket of hammer and saw, the talk was of the absent Admiral. Nelson had not been seen for a fortnight when the two concocted a pathetic message concerning the crying need for slops and bedding for their crew; a need which it was unnecessary to exaggerate, for it was only too true.

"If anything'll bring him, that will," Troubridge declared. "You know, Hardy, if glory comes first with Nelson the men come a good second. As for the ships," he added a trifle sourly, "it's you and me can look after them."

And Nelson came to Castellamare, without Lady Hamilton. To the anxious eyes of his captains he looked smaller, more pale and worn, than ever; but his old spirit seemed to well up in him as he watched the stepping of *Vanguard*'s foremast and afterwards sat in his old cabin taking wine with them. He had the Queen's promise, he assured Troubridge, that all their needs should be instantly supplied. He was disappointed with the progress of the repairs. He would ask Lady Hamilton—"the very best woman in the world, Hardy"—to urge King Ferdinand to take order with the dockyard; for he was impatient to take a squadron to Malta, which remained in the hands of the French.

"He's still the man we need, Hardy, in spite of them all," said Troubridge when he had gone. "And thanks be to God for it!"

"Amen to that," Hardy nodded. "The sooner we're ready for Malta the better."

"Aye. Once he's away from the painted monkeys up yonder —and that damned woman—we'll have a man to lead us again."

But *Culloden* was still without her rudder-pintles when the expedition sailed for Malta. *Vanguard* and six ships of the line reached Valetta in late October and Captain Hardy was in better humour with himself and the world than he had been for many a long week. His Admiral's pleasure at being at sea once again was so evident, his health so plainly improved by the passage, that Hardy clucked over him (as he told himself with indulgent scorn) like an old hen with one chick. On that brief voyage, indeed, the flag-captain was treated by the admiral very much as a son might treat his father, despite the fact that Nelson was now forty years of age and Hardy only thirty. Hardy was chiefly anxious lest the French garrison should defy the squadron and a prolonged siege ensue; he was as certain as ever that Nelson's belief in his genius for land operations was utterly unfounded. His anxiety was quickly to turn in another direction.

The French in fortified Valetta refused to surrender, though the garrison on Gozo, Malta's lesser island, capitulated under the threat of bombardment. But Nelson had no intention of landing guns and men for an attack on Valetta. Leaving Ball, his senior captain, in command of the squadron to blockade the port, he took *Vanguard* back to Naples. And there, once again, the glittering crowds in the villas and palace above the stinking rookeries of the port enveloped and swallowed him.

If Naples needed further excuse for bombastic jubilation she soon had it. There had now been time for the tidings of the Nile victory to reach England and for its repercussions to come back by fast frigate. The news had not only thrilled Englishmen from the highest to the lowest in the land, it had also saved the government and (most probably) the jobs of those Lordships who had chosen Nelson for the command. There was a peerage for the Admiral—he was Baron Nelson of the Nile and of Burnham Thorpe—with £2,000 a year and a gift of £10,000 from the East India Company; with jewels and orders from the Sultan of Turkey, from all the European royalties who were still on their thrones, from the lunatic Tsar of Russia. There were knighthoods for two of his captains and gold medals from King George for all the rest. Once more the banners and illuminations came out and the balls and parties succeeded each other night after night.

Captain Hardy, bedevilled yet again by anxiety, maintained ship routine and rigorous discipline on board an idle flagship. His anxiety was not concerned alone with the dangers that threatened the Admiral among what Troubridge had called "the painted monkeys". Nelson, on board for a busy day of paper-work in his cabin, had told him of the great project which he—abetted, it seemed, by the Queen of Naples and Lady Hamilton—was urging upon King Ferdinand. The Neapolitan Army, in theory 20,000 strong, was to be mustered and launched against the French army of 13,000 men at Castellana in Italy. Nelson himself had interviewed and approved the brilliant Austrian general, Mack, who was to lead the Neapolitans to victory. The Austrian emperor had undertaken to send an army from the north, 5,000 soldiers would be landed at Leghorn to advance from the west, and the French, outnumbered and caught between three fires, could either surrender or be annihilated. Hardy was not asked for his opinion of this plan but he gave it nevertheless.

"If this was a British army it might succeed," he said bluntly, "but I'd not depend on the Neapolitans if I were you, Sir Horatio."

"'My lord' is now correct, Hardy," Nelson said with the briefest of smiles. "Don't you see I'm forced to depend on the Neapolitans? I must strike at the French—I must bind the Two Sicilies to the British cause. And how can we fail, with odds of four to one in our favour?"

"I don't know, my lord, unless the four fail to attack the one."

The Admiral frowned and tugged impatiently at his empty sleeve. "We'll not discuss this further, Hardy, if you please.

I intend to sail by mid November at latest. *Vanguard* and *Culloden* will escort the army transports to Leghorn."

It was in fact November 28th when the 5,000 Neapolitans, with their horses, cannon, and stores, were landed at Leghorn. *Culloden* was left there, and *Vanguard* returned with the frigate *Alcmene* to Naples, where Nelson had at once rejoined the Hamiltons at the Palazzo Sessa.

Captain Hardy, staring out at the sea horizon in the pale December sunshine, considered all this and found it dispiriting. To his mind the bolstering-up of decaying Mediterranean kingdoms, the landing of dubious armies, was not a proper use of the Navy's ships or their admiral. Nelson's fatal conviction that he could do on land what he had done at sea was bound to get him into trouble, and so was his increasing preoccupation with that woman at the Palazzo Sessa. Hardy was dimly aware that his dislike of Emma Hamilton was founded mainly on a kind of jealousy, but she had angered him in other ways. Before *Vanguard*'s Leghorn voyage Nelson's flagship had been a fashionable raree-show for all the acquaintances of Lady Hamilton and Queen Maria Carolina, and after her return it had been the same. At first these titled visitors were armed with authorisations signed by the Admiral, but soon it was Emma who was signing them, and Emma who was demanding the full naval ceremony of "piping the side" for certain marquises and counts when they came on board. An appeal to Nelson by the exasperated Hardy only produced an almost apologetic request that her ladyship should be humoured in this, "since the Navy is so deeply in her debt". Hardy had had to conform, angrily conscious of the disapproval of his whole ship's company. His own disapproval showed itself in the minimum of hospitality he accorded to his jewelled and perfumed visitors; which they did not fail to report to Lady Hamilton. The culmination of this petty warfare had been the ignoring of Emma's intercession for the delinquent boat's crew. That she would complain to Nelson was certain, that Nelson would approve her attempt to interfere with naval discipline less so. But Hardy, who had watched the rapid increase of her influence over the Admiral during the past weeks was beginning to wonder just how far she would beguile him in the end.

A seaman trotted aft to the belfry and struck six bells of the afternoon watch. The captain of the *Vanguard* pushed Emma Hamilton out of his thoughts and went below to con over the purser's list of stores.

When Lord Nelson came on board his ship three days later, on December 18th, it was obvious that he had weightier matter to discuss with his flag-captain than the punishment of disorderly seamen. Hardy was shocked by his sickly pallor and the deep lines of worry on his thin face. He beckoned the captain peremptorily to follow him down to the day-cabin.

"Bad news, Hardy," he said as soon as the door was closed. "The worst. You heard the rumour, of course."

"I heard there'd been a battle, my lord. A victory for—" Hardy hesitated—"our army."

"The rumour lied. It was a French victory. The Neapolitans ran like rabbits at the first contact—every officer and man, and that scoundrel Mack with them."

Nelson sat down at the table and covered his face with his one hand. The news did not surprise Hardy in the least. If he felt concern it was for Nelson, who had clearly not allowed for any such disaster.

"Where's the French army now, my lord?" he asked.

The Admiral looked up wearily. "Less than a week's march from Naples and advancing fast. So says a dispatch from General Mack, just received by the King. He advises their majesties to fly at once. I know not what else they can do."

"It's not your—I should say their—intention to defend the port?"

"Totally impossible. There are no landward defences and the army is completely scattered." A faint flush tinged the hollow cheeks. "Never could I have thought it! What will they say in England?"

"Better to consider what we shall do now, my lord," Hardy said coolly. "The Royal family will embark for Sicily, I imagine?"

Nelson had sunk his head on his hand again, the picture of despair. The flag-captain's matter-of-fact tone seemed to rouse him a little.

"Not only the Royal family," he said dully, "but the whole court—and every person in Naples who has supported our cause, if they're to escape the guillotine. How am I to get them all away? I've only *Vanguard* and *Alcmene* here."

An instantaneous picture of his ship crowded with titled refugees passed through Hardy's mind with daunting effect but he concealed his misgivings.

"There's the *Samuel and Jane* and the two other transports we used for the Leghorn expedition, my lord," he said. "They're still here. There's the Portuguese ship, *Rainha de Portugal*. And surely the Neapolitan naval vessels—"

"Their crews won't leave this port. They refuse to desert their families when the French are coming."

"That's known to them, then?"

"Only suspected as yet. Deserters from the army have been coming in by thousands. But there's a larger problem, Hardy." Nelson clutched at his untidy mop of white hair. "My head, my head—I think it's splitting. Half the rabble of Naples are Jacobins, the other half won't let the King leave if they think he's deserting them. There's upwards of ninety thousand of these rogues and that's too many for us to defy openly. Get their majesties away I must—I'm responsible for their safety —*she* expects it of me!"

"We shall contrive something, my lord, never fear," said Hardy equably; that 'she', he thought, was not Queen Maria Carolina. "It's just a matter of bringing them off secretly." He tugged thoughtfully at this ear. "I recall a tale Captain

Troubridge told me. A tunnel or passage from the palace to the quays—"

"That's it, Hardy, that's it!"

Nelson was on his feet, his bright eye flashing. He looked twenty years younger.

"Lady Hamilton knows of it," he went on excitedly. "It leads to the Vittoria quay, behind the Figlio mole. There's our way—and we must waste not a moment." He sat down again, his meagre figure now tense and upright. "Pens and ink and paper, Hardy. We'll plan this now, and we'll keep the plan between the two of us."

The flag-captain got writing materials from a locker and pulled up a chair to the table. Nelson snatched a pen and dipped it, then paused, suddenly motionless, to stare rather oddly at the big man opposite him.

"Do you know, Hardy," he said slowly, "I believe if you and I were one man, that man might conquer the world."

Captain Hardy thought this remark nonsensical but naturally did not say so.

"Indeed, my lord?" he said impassively. "Well, now, there's more than enough work for two men before us. Shall we take *Vanguard* first? If I rig cots in the day cabins—"

The plans for the embarkation involved hours of work but they were completed there and then. The Admiral insisted on this, though he was so exhausted at the end of it that his original intention of sleeping ashore at the Palazzo Sessa was abandoned and he spent the night on board *Vanguard*; departing early next morning, however, in some anxiety lest his absence should have worried Lady Hamilton. Hardy, who was to await his signal, spent the next forty-eight hours hastily preparing his ship for a great swarm of passengers and conferring at intervals with Hope of the *Alcmene* frigate and with the captains of the other ships that were to be used for the evacuation. On the morning of the 21st he and Hope received duplicate messages:

"*Most Secret*

Three barges, and the small cutter of the Alcmene, *armed with cutlasses only, to be at the Vittoria at half-past seven o'clock tonight precisely. Only the barge of the* Vanguard *to be at the wharf, the others to lay on their oars at the outside of the rocks. The above boats to be on board the* Alcmene *before seven o'clock, under the direction of Captain Hope. Grapnells to be in the boats.*

All other boats of the Vanguard *and* Alcmene *to be armed with cutlasses, and the launches with carronades to assemble on board the* Vanguard, *under the direction of Captain Hardy, and to put off from her at half-past eight o'clock precisely, to row halfway towards the Mola Figlio. These boats to have 4 or 6 soldiers in them. In case assistance is wanted by me, false-fires will be burnt.*

NELSON"

Hardy perceived from this concise and careful message that his Admiral was himself again. He could stop worrying about Nelson and concentrate on the awkward operation ahead.

He was never to forget that December night. The stealthy emergence of file after file of cloaked and hooded figures from the secret tunnel, the packing of them all into the boats that shuttled between ships and quay, was accomplished without any alarm being given. The refugees' voluminous baggage, including two dozen casks full of golden ducats, had all been safely embarked during the day in the guise of ship's stores. The instrument of calamity was the weather. A long ground-swell had been running in the Bay all morning and at nightfall it increased, with a strong wind. The unfortunates crowded in the tossing barges were vomiting long before they reached the ships and half of them were incapable of getting on board unaided. The wallowings of *Vanguard* and the rest of the little fleet terminated the resistance of those who had managed to steady their stomachs thus far. As the flagship rose and plunged into the windy night on her course to weather Capri she was a pandemonium of noise and stink and mess, half comic and half tragic. Packed with Neapolitan aristocracy from wardroom to orlop, she resounded to the cries and screams of children, the groans and oaths of their elders, and the shouted adjurations of ship's officers and petty officers striving vainly to bring some measure of order into uncontrolled chaos.

There was no sleep for Captain Hardy or any of *Vanguard*'s people that night. Sea and wind rose higher when the flagship had rounded Capri and set her course for Palermo 150 miles away. Men and women rolled in the alleyways, screeching countesses demanded to be put on shore instantly, all the seasick valets and chambermaids were on their knees saying their last prayers. The King's Confessor, who was lucky enough to have a bunk, fell out of it and broke his arm, the Duchess of Castellamare fell against a sideboard and cut her head open. Hardy, striding everywhere, found two people whose coolheadedness and practical aid to all and sundry he could admire. One was Lord Nelson; the other, to his amazement, was Emma Hamilton. It was Emma who splinted the Confessor's arm, who bathed the foreheads of sick children, who made Nelson sit down and drink a glass of brandy. There was more to Lady Hamilton, he told himself, than he had thought.

It was in the howling dark of the middle watch that a furious squall blew *Vanguard*'s topsails to pieces and carried away her driver and foretopmast-staysail. Hardy, hurrying below after supervising the cutting-away of the wreckage, met Lady Hamilton coming along the alleyway at the foot of the companion-ladder. The light of a swinging lantern showed her face alive with laughter. She stopped when she saw Hardy, and then came on to halt him with a hand on his chest.

"I must tell someone, Hardy," she said, "and you'll do for want of a better. I've just been to my husband's cabin. I found Sir William sitting on his bed with a pistol in each hand. He says he'll blow his brains out rather than die with the guggle-guggle of salt water in his throat!—But you don't think that's funny? No, I didn't think you would. Tell me where I'll find some lemons for the Queen."

Hardy found her inexplicable. He thought her none the less dangerous for that.

It was pouring with rain when *Vanguard* dropped anchor within Palermo Mole at 2 a.m. of a pitch-black morning, but those on board her were as thankful as if they had arrived in heaven. And not least among these was her captain.

3

Captain Hardy's relief at reaching Palermo was short-lived. The long business of cleansing and repairing his ship was scarcely concluded when Nelson confided to him that he had written to Lord St Vincent resigning his command in the Mediterranean, with the request that *Vanguard* should be allowed to convey him and Sir William and Lady Hamilton to England. He felt he had not much longer to live, his health and his reputation were deteriorating, he was a useless invalid. Troubridge or Ball would be infinitely better in command.

Hardy received this news with his customary imperturbability and a grain of salt besides. He was beginning to know his Admiral. He had come to perceive that Horatio Nelson's was a many-sided personality despite the little man's transparent simplicity. There was the gifted naval commander and leader of men—and there was now no faltering in Hardy's belief in this side of him. There was the ailing, prematurely aged man, one-armed and half blind, waging a perpetual and heroic struggle with his disabilities; a figure demanding unbounded admiration. There was the morbidly sensitive person who fed upon the affection of everyone around him and could not exist without it. And there was the seeker after glory and advancement unable to suffer the least blow at his vanity or the least hint that his merits might go unrewarded. It was this last aspect of him, Hardy felt sure, that was to the fore now, and he had more than a suspicion that the "black fit" of depression had been brought on by the state of things ashore. In this he was soon proved right.

The problem of accommodating two thousand aristocratic Neapolitans, all accustomed to a life of luxury, in Palermo had been solved by distributing them among the many villas and palaces, many of which had been untenanted for years. By the insistence of their grateful majesties of the Two Sicilies, Nelson was installed in the vast but damp and chilly Villa Bastioni, some distance from the larger and even chillier Colli Palace where the Hamiltons were the guests of the King and Queen. The almost unlimited wealth of the refugees soon improved matters, however. Within a month a fair representation of the high-life in vogue at Naples was in full swing. The indefatigable Emma Hamilton had persuaded her "Sir Willum" to acquire the magnificent Palazzo Palagonia, Nelson moved in with them, and the unceasing round of dinner-parties, balls, and resplendent entertainments featuring Lady Hamilton's songs and classical attitudes began again. A brig from Gibraltar brought the expected letter from the Commander-in-Chief begging Lord Nelson not to resign a command which no one else could competently take over. And Lord Nelson, his equanimity restored and his pleasure-loving friends around him, was happy once again.

His flag-captain was not happy. He was idle and he detested idleness. Vanguard lay idle within the Palermo mole, and the Admiral, though hardly to be called idle, apparently preferred to conduct his naval business from inside the Palazzo Palagonia. His ships, except for the flagship, were busy enough. Ball with one squadron was blockading Malta, Troubridge with another had been sent from Leghorn to Naples to blockade that port and do what he could on the side of the royalists. Hardy was torn between two desires. Half of him would have given his post-captaincy to be at sea with one of the squadrons, the other half, uneasy about Nelson's involvement at the Palazzo, would not have left Palermo. He longed (nonsensically, he knew) for some superhuman despot with the power to pluck the Admiral from Lady Hamilton's side and dump him in the van of a British fleet with his face towards the enemy. It was about this time that a brig from Gibraltar arrived with the English mails, including a letter for Captain Hardy from Susan Manfield. Letter-writing was usually a laborious and uncongenial duty to Hardy, but on this occasion, feeling a desperate need to confide in someone, he wrote a long letter to Susan. There was hardly a word in it about himself or her. It was all about Horatio Nelson.

The English news was mainly concerned with Mr Pitt's unprecedented step of levying a direct tax on all incomes over £60 a year, rising to two shillings in the pound on those over £200. The war situation on the continent was improving, with Russians and Austrians winning back the conquests of the absent General Bonaparte; the French Revolutionary armies were outnumbered on every frontier, and there was talk of an expedition to drive the French out of Holland. Thinking it over later, Hardy concluded that it was this weakening of the French power in the north that made possible the astounding success of the Christian Army of the Holy Faith.

Naples had been the Parthenopean Republic since January. On the arrival of the French the customary slaughter of royalists and suspected royalists had duly taken place and the uneasy rule of liberty, fraternity, and equality was imposed. Most of King Ferdinand's loyal *lazzaroni* escaped to the south, and presently found themselves enlisted in an army consisting mainly of armed peasants and brigands and commanded jointly by the warlike Cardinal Ruffo and the arch-brigand known as Fra Diavolo. Austrian victories in Lombardy caused supporting French troops to be withdrawn from the neighbourhood of the Parthenopean Republic, and the Christian Army of the Holy Faith, 17,000 strong, marched on Naples. By the beginning of May the city and port were in the hands of Ruffo's men. Only the three forts, where the French garrison and their Neapolitan supporters had barricaded themselves, still held out. Troubridge and his four ships in Naples Bay were besieged by boatloads of triumphant banditti bringing what they claimed to be Neapolitan traitors for trial and execution.

Much of this Hardy heard from Troubridge when the two met at Naples at the end of June. At the time it was taking place he had suddenly become very busy.

Foudroyant, a fine 80-gun ship launched the previous year, arrived at Palermo to join Lord Nelson's command and it was (of course) necessary that the "Patroness of the Navy" should be shown over her by the Admiral. Lady Hamilton took a fancy to the new arrival. Whether as a result of this, as Hardy believed, or because *Foudroyant* carried more guns than his other ships, Nelson at once shifted his flag to the newcomer, taking Hardy and all *Vanguard*'s officers with him. Scarcely had this transfer been made when news reached Palermo that an enemy fleet, escaping the blockade, was in the Mediterranean and heading towards Naples. Hardy, hastily preparing the new flagship for sea at his Admiral's order, mentally rubbed his hands in glee; at last Nelson was to be rescued from that woman and placed, for a while at least, in his proper sphere. His glee was illusory. Collecting what ships he could at short notice, the Admiral cruised in search of the enemy. But he sought them only where they were likely to threaten the possessions of his royal protégés, and his almost hysterical anxiety lest they should slip past him to Palermo both saddened and exasperated his flag-captain. Whether or no Nelson really believed the preservation of the Sicilian kingdom to be vital to the British cause, it was only too evident to Hardy that his concern was for the inhabitants of the Palazzo Palagonia.

The cruise ended without sight or sign of the enemy. Admiral Bruix's raid into the Mediterranean had been abortive, and his ships had got out again through the straits and were safe in Cadiz harbour. A week later, on June 24th, *Foudroyant*, with Sir William and Lady Hamilton on board, anchored in Naples Bay.

Captain Hardy's phlegmatic exterior was no hollow mask. England and Dorset and his own thick skin had given him enormous reserves of endurance both physical and mental. The next three months, his last on the Mediterranean station, were to bring the hardest trials of his career and come close to ending that career altogether. Though he himself scarcely realised it, the armour of Stoic selfishness, in which he had cased himself since his youth, could protect him no longer. Hardy's growing affection for Nelson had made him more vulnerable than he knew.

Naples was in an uproar of bloodlust and revenge. How many innocents had been slaughtered in its streets by Cardinal Ruffo's royalist brigands was not known, but there were still hundreds of victims awaiting hangman or executioner—citizens and officials and nobles who had been forced to co-operate with the French or had merely failed to oppose them. Farcical trials (sometimes with the prisoner not present), mass executions, bribery, perjury, and intimidation were the adjuncts of Neapolitan justice, and the opportunity of swearing away the lives of rival tradesmen, suspected lovers, and unwanted husbands was freely taken. No less than seventy aristocratic families were being held in Troubridge's ships while their countrymen howled for their blood. Ruffo, sickened by this bloodbath, had offered terms to the Jacobin supporters in the forts, which now flew the white flag: they could march out with the honours of war and either return to their homes in Naples or depart by sea to Toulon. These terms were accepted.

Nelson entered this arena like an avenging angel. With sinking heart, Hardy perceived that the single-minded determination that could annihilate an enemy fleet knew nothing of mercy when it was applied to the unfortunates who had willy-nilly opposed King Ferdinand. Declaring that only the King's justice could deal with such traitors, the Admiral annulled the treaties with the forts. The men, women, and children who had embarked in the transports for Toulon were taken off and thrown into prison hulks or the gaols of Naples ("compared to which", Troubridge told Hardy, "death is a trifle") and the families who had returned to their homes were ordered to surrender themselves forthwith to the Neapolitan authorities. Day after day, week after week, the heads fell and the gallows groaned and hunted fugitives were dragged from their hiding-places. Commodore Francesco Carraciolo, who pleaded that he had been given the choice of serving the French or having his wife and family killed, was hanged at the yardarm of the Neapolitan flagship he had once commanded, while the crews of the British ships manned the yards for the occasion. Ten days after King Ferdinand's arrival from Palermo a group of leading Neapolitan collaborators noted by Troubridge as "princes, dukes, commoners and ladies" were executed. The height of the holocaust was past and the town ready to receive its pleasure-loving masters again. But the public executions in the Piazza del Mercato were to be a permanent feature of Naples entertainment for nearly a year to come.

Back to the villas and palaces came the lords and ladies and their innumerable servants. Out came the banners and coloured lights for the anniversary of the Nile on August 1st. Hymns to Nelson, his portrait supported by two angels on an illuminated boat, his image in wax carried round the streets. The vast rooms and galleries of the Palazzo Sessa thronged with junketing aristocracy once again, Emma Hamilton the liveliest and most Junoesque of hostesses. And, once again, Horatio Nelson in residence at the Palazzo with his dear friends the Hamiltons, newly created Duke of Brontë by his royal friend King Ferdinand of the Two Sicilies.

"They call 'em *tria juncta in uno*," Troubridge said bitterly, "and I'd say it's fact. If it is, Sir William's the most complacent cuckold you ever saw. Maybe he gets his share of Emma now and again—it wouldn't be often, at his age."

"Oh, come now, Troubridge," Hardy said uncomfortably.

"It's no uncommon arrangement among the gang up there, I assure you. They've less morals than my grandad's pigs in County Tyrone."

The two captains were sitting in Hardy's day-cabin on board *Foudroyant*. The last sunlight of a late September evening shone through the stern windows and sent a reflected gleam from the waters of Naples Bay to tremble on the deckhead above them. Troubridge was in full-dress uniform. He had been to a reception at the Palazzo Sessa and had left early, unable (as he said) to stand another minute of it.

"They were cramming the card-room when I left, all half-drunk and all yelling and shrieking at the tops of their voices, which is what they call conversation." Troubridge nodded thanks as Hardy poured brown Marsala into his glass. "Emma doing the mighty over everyone and our poor Nelson tucked into her armpit."

"How did he look?" Hardy asked.

"You'd think he was dying, until Emma lets out one of her horse-laughs and he gives a bit of a smile. Tcha!" *Culloden*'s captain took a gulp of wine. "Our conquering hero. Dear, dear Nelson. My lord, pray wear this diamond ring for me. He just sits there quietly and accepts it all, as if he was far above all of them. I heard one woman call him 'our Saviour' and he nodded at her without a smile. By God, he *is* far above 'em all—but not as far as that!"

Hardy frowned. "Would you say he's beginning to think he is?"

"That's my fear, Hardy. Ball fears the same. You know he's twice refused to obey Keith's order?"

"Yes," said Hardy; Lord Keith had taken St Vincent's place as Commander-in-Chief at Gibraltar.

Troubridge sighed heavily. "He's heading for ruin. We've

done what we could. I told him plain, last week, that he should send a squadron to Minorca as Keith orders. 'If you don't, my lord,' I said, 'you'll lose your command here, sure as eggs is eggs.'"

"What did he say to that?"

"Why, I got a lightning-flash out of that one eye and then he wagged his head at me as if I was a naughty child. 'I know that Naples is more important than Minorca, Troubridge,' he says, 'and Lord Keith doesn't.' And that was that."

Hardy remembered Culverhouse of the *Minerve*. "He's never wrong," he said slowly.

"And it's human to err," said Troubridge. "That's what Ben Hallowell had in mind when he sent Nelson a coffin made from *Orient*'s mainmast. But the root of all the mischief, Hardy, is Emma Hamilton."

"I know it."

"It's she who's persuaded him he's a little god. If he could but be convinced that he owes it to his country to cast off from her—duty was ever a word of power with him. I wonder—" Troubridge hesitated. "How often does he come aboard *Foudroyant*?" he went on abruptly.

"Generally once in a week. It's ten days now since he came on board last."

"Then you could be seeing him tomorrow or the next day." The eyes of the two men met and held steadily. "There's no one he'd take it better from than you, Hardy," said Troubridge, "but his broadside's heavier than yours."

"I'll risk it," Hardy said briefly.

"You're a brave man. Here's luck to you." Troubridge drained his glass, set it down, and stood up. "That wine's the only good thing that ever came out of Sicily."

Hardy saw him over the side into his gig and then took a turn or two on *Foudroyant*'s quarterdeck. He looked more than once across the sunset-reddened water to where the elderly frigate *Princess Charlotte* lay at anchor. He thought of an

Admiralty message received a few days ago notifying the departure for the Mediterranean of the *Bulldog* sloop-of-war with Captain Sir Edward Berry a passenger on board. When he went below again his mind was made up.

At noon next day Rear-Admiral Lord Nelson sat at a table in his flagship's stern cabin and Captain Thomas Hardy stood facing him.

"I ask your lordship's permission to speak plainly."

"You always speak plainly, Captain Hardy."

There was no trace of a smile on Nelson's thin face as he made that reply. From beneath its drooping lid his good eye watched the other's expressionless countenance warily.

"This time it's not on my own account, my lord. There are many besides myself who would tell you this." The words came out slowly and with deliberation. "A man as highly placed as yourself, with the eyes of the Navy and the world upon you, can't afford to behave as you're behaving, my lord. I beg you to consider the bad effect it must have on ships and men, not to mention their Lordships at home." Hardy found himself speaking more easily. "I've heard you say that England confides that every sea-officer will do his duty, which is to obey orders as well as give them, my lord. You never failed to practise what you preach until—until a year ago."

"Have you done?" said Nelson in a low unsteady voice as he paused.

"No, my lord. If I'm to be honest with you, I've to say what all of us know who have any sort of care for your lordship. You stay inactive here, at a foreign court, from no motive of duty. It's plain enough you're in a bondage—"

"Be careful, Hardy!" said the Admiral in the same low voice.

Hardy lost patience and with it his *my lords* and formal utterance. He bent forward with his knuckles resting on the table and let his words come from the heart.

"Scrounch it all, man, it's you that needs to be careful!

Are you fool enough to spite your country for a woman? Will you make a higgle of your life for a woman, another man's wife—"

"That's enough!"

Nelson was on his feet, his face dead white and his eye flashing. Before that fiery glare the flag-captain fell back a pace and stood stiffly erect. The Admiral's shrill voice lashed him.

"You forget your rank, Captain Hardy! I'll not suffer this from you or any man—leave this cabin instantly!"

Hardy stood his ground. "My lord—"

"By God, I'll take order with you, Hardy!"

"A year ago you promised me a frigate, my lord. I claim the promise now."

Nelson sat down suddenly in his chair. His chin sank on his chest and he looked so utterly weary and forlorn that Hardy had great difficulty in going on.

"The *Princess Charlotte* goes home for refitting, my lord," he said steadily. "I believe Sir Edward Berry will reach Naples in the coming week."

Try as he might he could get no farther. The Admiral had taken a pen and was writing, his left hand moving jerkily across the paper, his untidy white head bent above it. He spoke in a voice so low that it was barely audible.

"Your appointment to the *Princess Charlotte* shall be made tomorrow."

"Thank you, my lord."

Hardy waited a moment but Nelson did not look up. He turned on his heel and went out of the cabin.

4

There was snow on Black Down that Christmas but none on the Dorset lanes that wandered above the coast and the long Chesil Bank. Portisham village (known to its inhabitants as Possum) surprised Captain Hardy with an ovation; at least, that was how the *Weymouth Intelligencer* described four dozen cheering schoolchildren, a laborious speech by the beadle, and a banner with WELCOME on it stretched across the village street from the Blue Lion to Mother Groby's cake-shop. There were also two fiddles and a serpent waiting to play the appropriate tune for a Conquering Hero when he got down from the Abbotsbury stage-coach. Hardy thought of Naples and Palermo and liked this reception the better for that memory.

The *Princess Charlotte* had paid off a month ago. He had duly reported to Admiralty and had been coldly informed that he was unlikely to be appointed to another command for some time. He had spent ten minutes closeted with Lord Spencer himself and had stolidly parried the First Lord's guarded but acute questions concerning Lord Nelson. He had gone with Spencer to be presented to the King, who had been adequately gracious in his own curt explosive way but had avoided all mention of Nelson. He had twice been recognised and cheered in the streets of London. It was borne in upon Hardy that while the name of Nelson had become legendary among the folk of England it was a name of ill omen in high quarters. Nelson's flag-captain was assured of respect and admiration wherever he went—except at Whitehall and Windsor.

He spent Christmas with his numerous family. His elder brother Jos and his new-wedded wife had come to join his younger brother, five sisters, and their stout and ageing parents; Catherine was now married to John Manfield of Elworth. They were all glad to see him, proud of his rapid advancement and the reflected glory that was his because of Nelson. But they were not much interested in the Navy, or (except for the doings of the local Volunteers) in the war, and after the first somewhat perfunctory questions about his visits to foreign parts the talk returned to Dorset and family matters. It had always been a sort of tradition with the Hardys, a widespread tribe in that county, to keep a number of family quarrels going, and the current development of these was the prime subject of conversation among the Portisham branch. Captain Hardy felt out of it. He had hoped to install himself as Tom Hardy of Portisham once more, and in so doing to rid himself of the strange sense of incompleteness that had bothered him since he had parted from Nelson two months ago; but he was no longer at home in Dorsetshire.

On the day after Boxing Day he rode over to Elworth to take afternoon dinner with the Manfields. He had been mildly surprised, though not greatly disappointed, that Susan Manfield had not been there with his family to greet him. The discouraging hints he had received at the Admiralty about future employment had strengthened his decision to take a wife, and he had gone so far as to discuss with Jos the purchase of a suitable property where he and Susan might live in reasonable comfort and style.

It was more than three years since he had last seen Susan and he hardly recognised the self-possessed young lady who gave him her hand when he crossed the threshold of his brother-in-law's house. Hardy kissed the hand, and might have ventured a more intimate salute if Catherine and her husband had not been present. John Manfield, gentleman as well as solicitor, took a keen interest in the progress of the war both on land and at sea, and since he had the knack of "drawing-out" anyone in conversation Hardy found himself talking at the Manfields' table as he had never talked in his own home. He had always liked John, whose quick understanding could meet his own difficulty of expression halfway, and his usual taciturnity was flung aside. It was dark outside when the time came to take his leave, and candles were alight in the entrance hall. Perhaps by some prior arrangement, John and Catherine had made their adieux in the parlour and it was Susan who came out with him to the hall.

"Fred's bringing your horse round, Captain Hardy," she

said in that new, very cool voice of hers. "Time enough for the little I have to say, which is this. If you're thinking of offering for me, pray don't. I thank you for the honour but I don't want you."

Hardy, who had made to embrace her, dropped his arms to his sides. He could think of nothing to say.

"I know you don't love me, you see," she went on calmly. "I knew it, truly, that day in Portsmouth when we said goodbye, but I was only a girl then. I was sure of it when I got that letter, all Nelson and nothing else. And today. We've not seen each other for three years and it's been Nelson this and Nelson that all the time you've been in this house. There's Fred outside with your horse now."

"But Susan—" Hardy groped for words. "It was agreed upon—I've been in love with you since we were children."

"Oh, no." She opened the outer door. "It won't do, Captain Hardy. If you're in love with anyone it's with Nelson. Goodbye —Tom!"

The door closed upon her. Captain Hardy climbed into the saddle and rode slowly away, puzzling over the extraordinary ways of womenfolk. *In love with Nelson*—a nonsensical thing to say. The words had no meaning. It was true he had a fondness for the little Admiral despite his silliness. Nelson had sent him packing and so had Susan, but he would go on missing Nelson, and he wouldn't miss Susan Manfield at all. Come to think of it, his feeling just now was not so much of regret as of release. He kicked his horse's sides and went down the dark lane at a lively trot.

FIVE

1

The first year of a new century was disastrous for England. General Bonaparte, having routed an army of 15,000 Turks landed from British ships at Aboukir, had marched back to Paris and made himself First Consul of France. His subsequent master-strokes had been far too swift and adroit to be countered by a British Government that was both inept and divided; attempts to send the British army by sea to half-a-dozen threatened points resulted in what Lord Cornwallis called "twenty-two thousand men floating round the greater part of Europe, the scorn and laughing-stock of friends and foes." On every front the Austrian armies, fighting alone, were beaten by the French. And while Bonaparte in person led 33,000 men to victory at Marengo, regaining for France the advantage that had been lost at the Battle of the Nile, Lord Nelson and the Hamiltons were making a leisurely progress homeward, pausing to be fêted and applauded in the European capitals that were not yet threatened by the French.

The year was disastrous at home, too. The storm-battered ships and their weary crews still blockaded the French and Spanish navies in their ports, enabling food and supplies to reach Britain; but bread, the staple food, was dangerously scarce. An unprecedented drought followed by torrential rains had ruined the harvest. Grain imported from the Baltic states suddenly trebled the price of bread, the poor in towns and villages faced starvation, and bread riots had to be quelled by the military. On the horizon lowered an even darker prospect, for the First Consul's diplomacy was drawing Russia, Sweden and Denmark into a League of Armed Neutrality that would cut off from Britain the spar timber she needed for her hundreds of ships as well as the grain essential to her life. It was in an England beset by apprehension that Captain Hardy endured an inactive twelve months.

A sea-captain without a ship, Hardy found it impossible to settle down and wait for a summons from the Admiralty. In any case, he knew that he had little chance of employment for some time to come; there were more post-captains than ships for them to command and there were a dozen who would be chosen before him to fill any vacancy. Spring at Portisham in the bosom of his quarrelsome family had few attractions and he found respectable lodgings in London within reasonable walking distance of Fladong's Coffee House. "Coffee-housing" was a primary occupation of unemployed naval officers and Fladong's was the traditional rendezvous of post-captains. Not only was it the meeting-place of old acquaintances and the likeliest place to hear of possible employment, but also a fount of the latest news from the theatres of war. Hardy spent a great deal of his time there. But early in the period of his London residence he went to 54 St James's Street to pay his respects to Lady Nelson, who had rented a house for herself and her husband's old and ailing father.

That first visit was a brief one. The plain, self-possessed woman of middle-age who had been Fanny Nisbet welcomed Nelson's one-time flag-captain with moderate warmth and asked just those questions which might be expected from a wife who had not seen her husband for two years. That she knew of the liaison with Emma Hamilton was certain; London was buzzing with gossip about the two, ill-informed and therefore exaggerated. But Lady Hamilton's name did not pass Lady Nelson's lips and Hardy did not take it upon himself to mention her. Nelson's wife enlisted his sympathy and respect by her fortitude, but he saw only too clearly that her air of patient martyrdom stood no chance at all, where Horatio Nelson was concerned, against Emma Hamilton's tempestuous affection.

For the ageing Rector of Burnham Thorpe Hardy conceived an equal sympathy. The small whitehaired old man possessed his son's childlike simplicity without Nelson's fiery spirit, and his pride in his famous son was as evident as his utter guilelessness. Discovering that the Rector's exile from the Norfolk countryside had deprived him of certain delicacies on which he doted, Hardy on his next visit to Portisham sent a present of ducklings and seakale to the house in St James's Street.

At Fladong's he learned in August that Lord Nelson had been relieved of his Mediterranean command and was on his way home, travelling overland (it was said) by Lady Hamilton's insistence. Hardy sought eagerly for news of him and week by week it came, together with drops and driblets of gossip: of the interminable progress from Court to Court across Europe, of Nelson—"a perfect gig, all ribbons and orders"—lapping up the adulation shamelessly demanded for him by Lady Hamilton, of "Antony and his Moll-Cleopatra" embarking on the Elbe for the last part of their journey to Cuxhaven. London tittered and circulated bawdy jests. The cartoonist Gillray published near-libellous drawings in which the fair Emma's undoubtedly abundant charms were swollen to the point of monstrosity. At Fladong's and elsewhere Hardy found himself continually defending Nelson against detractors, flatly denying scurrilous rumours, even—as opposition roused his dogged loyalty—trying to present Lady Hamilton as a sort of motherly nurse with no sexual attraction for the Admiral. It was a painful rôle for him and his honest nature unfitted him for it. He became silent and sullen, resentful of an attachment which forced him to defend a man whose behaviour he himself considered indefensible.

In early November he was at the house in St James's Street

again, summoned thither by Lady Nelson's footman. She received him with the briefest of greetings and he saw at once that she was greatly agitated. Her cool composure when they met before had given him the impression of a woman older than her forty-two years; today, with her plain features softened by emotion, she looked ten years younger.

"It was kind of you to come, Captain Hardy. Will you—please read this."

Hardy took the paper she gave him, recognising as he did so the spidery left-handed scrawl.

Yarmouth

"*My dear Fanny,*

We are at this moment arriv'd and the post only allows me to say that we shall set off tomorrow noon, and be with you on Saturday, to dinner. I have only had time to open one of your letters, my visits are so numerous. May God bless you and my dear father, and believe me ever your affectionate

Brontë Nelson of the Nile

Sir and Lady Hamilton beg their best regards and will accept your offer of a bed."

"So he's here, in England!" Hardy said with pleasure, forgetting for a moment his own resentment and Lady Nelson's situation.

"Yes, he's here," she echoed.

Something in her tone made him eye her sharply. The faint colour was in her cheeks, her lips trembling in a half-smile. She was in love with him still; he had not thought that, and the realisation made him more sorry for her than ever. Feeling his glance upon her, she instantly regained her composure.

"Saturday is tomorrow," she said almost briskly. "And I've no one to advise me save you. Captain Hardy, are they—is she—"

She could not go on. Hardy averted his glance.

"If you're asking is she his mistress, ma'am," he said heavily, "I can't tell you, because I don't know."

"I understand. But I believe I may be certain of it." Her voice was quite steady. "His letters, few as they are, have told me. Not in words," she added quickly as he looked up in surprise, "but in the way he has written of her. Nelson is quite incapable of concealing anything like that. Now, Captain Hardy, you see how I am placed. This woman is to come here and I am to offer her and Sir William a bed. She and I and Nelson are to be under the same roof—for how long I am not told. What am I to do?"

Captain Hardy looked at her and away from her, tugged at his ear, scrubbed a big hand through his hair, and finally burst into speech.

"Scrounch me if I know, ma'am! You'll forgive me, but this is clean outside my experience."

"But you know Nelson. You're fond of him. And you've met this—this woman."

"That's right enough," Hardy said bluntly, "but I don't know you, ma'am. That's to say, I don't know what's passing in your mind."

"I would do a very great deal to bring him back to me," said Lady Nelson in a low voice.

"And I wish I could help you to that." The captain fingered his chin, frowning. "There's this to it. You're a lady and she isn't. He's never seen the two of you together, and when he does he can't help but see that. There's your course, ma'am."

She bit her lip. "I am to receive the Hamiltons as honoured guests? And Nelson as if—as if nothing had happened?"

"Just that. I'd say it's your best point of sailing, ma'am." Hardy paused, suddenly appalled at his own temerity. "But I'm sure of this, that he's very far gone. It's long odds against any advice of mine fetching him out of the tangle he's in. Pray remember I'm a bachelor, and a seaman at that, with nothing in his head but spars and cordage—"

"I do remember," she interrupted with a faint smile, "and I thank you. In any case, I see no course for me except the one you have pointed out. I shall follow it. You will not be to blame if I am wrecked in the end."

Hardy took the hand she held out to him and gripped it for some moments while he fumbled for words. "You're a damned brave woman, ma'am," he blurted out at last, and got out of the house rather faster than politeness would have admitted.

In St James's Street (to the amusement of some passing exquisites, who thought him drunk) he relieved his feelings with a string of oaths. Then he made his way with great strides to Fladong's and the pint of wine required for the dispelling of his vapours. One thing he had firmly resolved upon before he returned to his lodging : he would not show his face at the house in St James's Street again. Nor, after what had passed at their last meeting, would he seek out Nelson, despite his ineradicable desire to see the little Admiral again. In the event, it was Nelson who sought out Hardy.

It was a November evening at Fladong's and the main coffee-room was thronged and noisy with conversation. Most of the talk was of Admiral Lord Nelson's arrival in London, the cold reception rumoured to have been given him by the King, the chances of his ever holding a high command again. Hardy, taking coffee in an obscure corner with a middle-aged captain from Bridport, heard the buzz of talk cease abruptly, to be succeeded by a murmur through which a high imperious voice cut as clear as a trumpet.

"Hardy!" Nelson came thrusting through the crowd with left hand outstretched. "Hardy, my friend! This is a happy meeting—they told me I'd find you here."

His face, as thin and worn as ever, was flushed and smiling, his good eye alight with pleasure. He was wearing dress uniform, with the medals and ribbons of his orders. It was impossible to remember the angry exchange in *Foudroyant*'s stern cabin, impossible not to respond to that simple warmth.

Hardy grasped the thin little claw and smiled back, trying to find the right words.

"My lord—"

"Never mind that for a moment. I'm in haste." Nelson interrupted himself to make perfunctory introduction of the tall elderly man who had come in with him. "Mr Alexander Davison of Lincoln's Inn. We are bidden to dine with the First Lord.—Hardy, you're to dine with the Lord Mayor tomorrow, and I'll take no excuses. I'm the guest of honour at his Banquet and I told them they needn't expect to see me unless you were there. You'll be expected—don't fail! We'll talk another time."

He turned on his heel without waiting for whatever Hardy might say and with Davison behind him made for the door, the throng of men opening before him. The murmur swelled into a roar of approbation, almost a cheer, as he reached the door. The Admiral paused to acknowledge it, his deeply-lined face twisted into a grin of delight. Then he was gone.

Captain Hardy was at the Lord Mayor's Banquet and much relieved to find himself seated at a table a long way from the centre of the festivities. Rear-Admiral Lord Nelson was in high spirits. His carriage had been dragged by a vociferous crowd from Ludgate Hill to the Guildhall doors; in the Great Hall he was conducted to a seat under a triumphal arch. After the City Chamberlain's oration, the Admiral drew and held aloft the sword ("of the value of two hundred guineas") voted to him by the City, declaring in ringing tones that he would soon use it to reduce Britain's enemies to their proper place.

It was something of a naval occasion, Hardy noticed. Old Jervis was there—Earl St Vincent, First Lord of the Admiralty now—at the Lord Mayor's table with Nelson; so was a new Lord of the Admiralty, Sir Thomas Troubridge, a baronet these twelve months. Among Hardy's table companions was a likeable frigate captain, Blackwood by name, and what with good talk, good food, and good drink he passed the evening very pleasantly despite his dislike of formal dinners. He had no expectation of exchanging so much as a word with Nelson or Troubridge, far away across the glittering throng beneath the great chandeliers, nor was he able to do so. But when the feast was over and the crowd was shuffling noisily towards the great doors a powdered footman came wriggling through to place a folded paper in his hand. Hardy managed to read it as he was borne along with the departing revellers. The spidery scrawl was nearly indecipherable:

"I am to be employed again. You are to be my flag-captain. Take this as certain. Nelson."

2

"It's putting a blood mare in harness with a cart-horse," Troubridge said impatiently, "and so I tell 'em. But you'd as soon shift a sow from a cesspit as move some of my fellow Lordships." His brown eyes shot a quick glance at Captain Hardy. "You're the one man I'd talk to like this, Hardy. I know it won't go outside this room."

Hardy nodded. The small room at the back of the Admiralty offices, where the two were conferring, overlooked the leafless trees in St James's Park, where a pale February sunlight just penetrated the thin fog.

"Sir Hyde Parker's sixty-two," Troubridge went on, "and dotes on two things—his belly and his bride. She's eighteen and he don't fancy leaving her. I know, for he told me so, that he thinks Nelson too reckless a man to hold command."

"It's a bad lookout, sure," Hardy said.

"It was a bad decision. If they'd done as I wanted and given Nelson sole command—" Troubridge checked himself and leaned across the table, wagging a forefinger for emphasis. "This Baltic business is vitally important, Hardy. If the Armed League cuts off our timber and wheat we're as good as finished.

The Danes have broken their treaty with us and they're waiting to see what we'll do about it. No doubt Bonaparte, who put 'em up to it, told them England wouldn't dare send a battle fleet and risk Russia and Sweden coming in against her. Well, the Channel Fleet's sailing for the Baltic in three weeks, as you know, and its task is to strike swift and hard at Copenhagen."

"Nelson's the man for that."

"And Parker isn't. And he's the senior, for all that they're both vice-admirals now." Troubridge sighed. "I suppose the Machiavels who devised this thought Nelson would spur Parker on, and Parker would rein Nelson in, and the result would be a steady canter."

Hardy frowned. "The result could be a bad fall."

"Say a bad falling-out and you're hitting the mark," said Troubridge earnestly. "It's to make sure you were aware of the danger that I asked you to come and see me. If the vice-admiral in command falls foul of his second, or t'other way round, it means disaster for the Fleet. I say nothing," he added, "of what it would mean for Nelson. You know he and Lady Nelson have separated?"

"Yes."

"That's done him no good with the powers that be," Troubridge muttered. "But that's beside the point, which is that I'm asking you to avert that disaster if it threatens."

"I'm no diplomat, Sir Thomas," Hardy said slowly.

"Please to leave out the 'Sir'. I know you're no diplomat, Tom, but I know what you are. You'll do your best."

Hardy got to his feet. "I'll do that," he said.

On that they parted. Captain Hardy returned to Portsmouth, where Lord Nelson's flagship, the three-decker *St George*, was being hastily made ready for sea. His mind was full of dark forebodings; and he was soon to see them justified.

Yarmouth was the port of muster for the Baltic expedition,

and on arriving there Nelson went at once to call on his senior Admiral, taking Hardy with him. Sir Hyde Parker was a shortish, fattish, elderly man whose speech and movements were slow and deliberate. He would divulge nothing of his orders, or of his plans for carrying them out, to his second-in-command; he saw no reason for undue haste and did not propose to sail for another ten days—indeed, his wife was busy making arrangements for a farewell ball on March 13th, at which he hoped Lord Nelson and Captain Hardy would be present. At one point during this polite but cold interview Nelson's growing exasperation was clearly about to erupt in angry speech; Hardy, who stood close to him, was overtaken by a prolonged and thunderous fit of coughing and the danger passed. But—

"He's blind, Hardy, if he can't see that delay could mean defeat!" fumed Nelson as the gig pulled back to the *St George*. "By God, I'll take order with him, senior admiral or no!"

His method of doing this was to send an express messenger to Earl St Vincent. And in forty-eight hours the First Lord's order to put to sea forthwith was in Admiral Parker's hands. Whether or not he suspected what had happened, Sir Hyde made no communication to Nelson except by signal; when eighteen sail-of-the-line and thirty-five smaller vessels put to sea on March 12th the second-in-command of this fleet had not been informed, officially, whither it was bound.

Captain Hardy, seeing no way of bettering this sad state of affairs, was as gloomy as the weather, which was gloomy indeed. For the first few days the ships rolled and yawed dangerously in a freezing fog, through which light and capricious airs puffed uselessly. As in several of the other vessels, the flagship's hands rigged fishing-lines overside, a practice winked at by most captains because it provided a valuable addition to the crews' diet. Hardy would normally have forbidden it in a ship where he was flag-captain, and it was a symptom of his dispiritedness that he agreed when the request was made to him through his first lieutenant, Lyne. On the fifth day, still over the Dogger Bank, he heard without interest that a seaman named Jacobs had caught a magnificent turbot, as big as any man aboard had seen. That same day a northerly breeze dispelled the fog and grew to a gale, and the ships were able to head for the Skaggerak at a reasonable speed. But the wind brought snow and sleet. Ice glistened on the rigging before the long low headland of the Skaw, northernmost tip of Denmark, was sighted on the starboard bow through the drifting snow-showers. Admiral Parker signalled such of his ships as were in sight to heave-to; he was anxious to muster all his straggling Fleet before heading south into the Kattegat.

Hardy had seen very little of Nelson during the six days that had passed at sea. For half of that time the seasickness that always beset the Admiral at the beginning of a voyage had kept him below in the care of his servant, Tom Allen, and he had spent the last three days in his cabin studying charts and writing letters—letters, Hardy guessed, to Emma Hamilton. As the flag-captain walked his slippery quarterdeck with the icy spray pattering on his tarpaulin coat he had pondered many times on his present relationship with Horatio Nelson. Each time the result was the same: puzzled astonishment that his affection for Nelson was unchanged and his loyalty to him firmer than ever. No word had passed between them concerning the angry parting at Naples. On the one occasion when the Admiral had mentioned Lady Hamilton Hardy's disapproval had been unconcealed, but the only consequence was that her name was never spoken between them again. It was odd, to Hardy's way of thinking, that when all hope of a reconciliation with Fanny Nelson, who had enlisted his sympathy and help, had finally ended he should devote himself to the man who had cast her off. He could only admit to himself that his immediate anxieties were all on Nelson's account.

Those anxieties came to a head when Admiral Parker's flagship, the *London*, made the signal to heave-to off the Skaw.

When the signal was reported to him Nelson came on deck. The aggressive jut of his underlip, the smouldering fire in his one good eye, told Hardy what was coming.

"Call the gig away, Hardy," he said abruptly. "This has gone on long enough. We're in enemy waters and I've been told nothing—nothing! I'm going on board the Admiral. You'll come with me."

Hardy knew better than to protest; but he foresaw the angry accusations that could not be passed over, the fatal rift in command of which Troubridge had warned him. While Nelson went to his cabin to be attired in pea-jacket and boat-cloak, he summoned Lyne, ordered the gig slung outboard, and sent the first lieutenant for'ard with a message and a half-sovereign. He had remembered something else Troubridge had said.

The gig splashed and bucketed across the grey-green Baltic waves and sheered in below *London*'s cliff-like side. It was no easy task to board, but as usual Nelson refused assistance and went up one-handed to the deck. Hardy, following close behind, also climbed one-handed; he was carrying a long and heavy parcel wrapped in oiled canvas. On the quarterdeck a hastily-mustered reception party awaited them. Bosuns' pipes squealed, two ranks of marines presented muskets. Sir Hyde Parker, looking not at all pleased by this unasked visit, came across the deck towards them.

"I was not aware, my lord," he said coldly, "of any necessity for you to come aboard here."

Hardy, a pace behind his Admiral, saw the instant stiffening of Nelson's spine and the upward jerk of his chin. He stepped forward with his parcel, the picture of an awkward subordinate obeying his senior's order at the wrong moment, and loosed his powerful voice before Nelson could utter a single fiery word.

"His lordship begs your acceptance of a gift for your table, Sir Hyde. It's a fine turbot, caught on the Dogger."

Perhaps fortunately, he could not see his lordship's face.

Parker's glance had gone instantly to the parcel Hardy held out.

"A turbot!" he repeated pleasedly. "There's no tastier fish, rightly cooked. This was—ah—a kindly thought, my lord. Mr Ballard! See that this fish is delivered to my steward instantly, and be careful with it."

A very elegant lieutenant, wrinkling his nose in distaste, came forward and took the odiferous package from Hardy. Sir Hyde turned to Nelson.

"I—ah—intended to request your lordship's presence on board *London* at—ah—a later time," he said, displaying some embarrassment. "But no time like the present.—Captain Mainwaring, see that Captain Hardy has some refreshment.—Come down to my cabin, my lord. No time like the present, eh?"

An hour later Hardy, with a quantity of Mainwaring's excellent brandy inside him, was sitting beside Nelson in the sternsheets of the gig as she pulled back to *St George*. The Admiral's thin face peering out of the hood of his boat-cloak wore a more cheerful expression than it had done for a week past. He did not speak until they were halfway across.

"I've got my shoulder to the wheel at last, Hardy," he said then, suddenly. "It will be hard to turn but I'll do it."

His only other remark was made as the gig drew alongside *St George* and he made ready to board her. He flashed an impish smile at the flag-captain as he spoke.

"It's the first time I've heard of fish-oil being used to ease a wheel."

But the analogy would not hold, unless Nelson could be thought of as pushing Sir Hyde Parker's ships up a very steep hill. On the sea-plain of the Kattegat with the wind fair for the Sound and Copenhagen there was nothing to prevent the attack being made without delay; the passage of the Sound, 2½ miles wide between Sweden and Denmark, held a trifle of risk, but the Swedish forts at Elsinore were unlikely to fire on

British ships and by keeping to that side of the strait the Fleet would be beyond the range of the guns of Kronenburg, the Danish fortress. Yet Admiral Parker dillied and dallied, sailed his ships to the entrance of the Great Belt passage and back, and finally decided to go through the Sound. There had been a council-of-war on board *London* on March 23rd at which Nelson had not only pressed for an immediate passage of the Sound but had also propounded a detailed plan for the attack on Copenhagen and the Danish fleet in its harbour, a plan which Parker had declared to be rash but had not totally rejected. On the 30th the eighteen ships of the line, the eleven frigates, and the two dozen smaller vessels passed through the Sound, receiving no damage from the futile fire of the Kronenburg fort, and anchored five miles north-west of Copenhagen. Nelson, never a man to tolerate inertia once he had overcome it, at once swept Admiral Parker off for a reconnaissance in the *Skylark* lugger.

The Danish capital stretched along the low coast beyond the discoloured water over the Middle Ground shoal, the tower of Christiansborg Castle and the gilded dome of the Frederikskirke conspicuous against the wintry afternoon sky. Like a serrated black wall protecting the long line of the waterfront, Danish ships-of-the-line interspersed with floating batteries were moored, their mile-long rank marking the landward edge of the King's Channel leading to the narrow harbour entrance. Behind them broad mud-flats lay between ships and shore; in front of them, across the restricted soundings of the King's Channel, the wide Middle Ground shoal prevented direct approach from seaward and held hostile ships out of range. The city was safe from threat of bombardment so long as that wall of guns, impossible to avoid, held the King's Channel. Moreover, only the British ships of lighter draught could hope to navigate the Channel. All this Nelson recounted to Hardy on his return from the reconnaissance, together with his plan of attack, to which Admiral Parker had agreed. It was the final draft of the rough plan he had made before the Fleet passed the Sound, which had resulted (somewhat to his surprise) in Captain Hardy making that brief voyage as a passenger.

"I shall lead the dozen ships of lightest draught," Nelson had said. "*St George* won't do, Hardy. *Elephant* draws nearly two fathoms less, so I shall shift my flag to her."

"I hope you'll shift me too, my lord."

"That won't do either. Foley must act as flag-captain in his own ship."

"Then allow me to serve as volunteer in *Elephant*, my lord."

Nelson had laughed and clapped him on the shoulder. "Bravo, Hardy! You sail through every problem. But you'll have little to do—except to endure the hottest fire you've ever seen."

"I'd prefer to be with you," Hardy had said quietly.

Thus it came about that he was present in *Elephant*'s stern cabin on the evening of April 1st, the day before the battle.

The meal to which Nelson had bidden his chief captains was over. It had been a later dinner than usual, for at dusk his squadron of twelve of the line and five frigates had dropped down the Outer Channel to the tail of the Middle Ground, leaving Admiral Parker and the remainder of the ships anchored four miles to northward. Candlelight, and the yellow glow of a lantern hanging from the deckhead, shone on blue coats and white breeches and glinted from the gilt of buttons and epaulettes. Foley and Fremantle were there, Rear-Admiral Graves who was Nelson's second-in-command, Murray of the *Edgar*, Inman, Riou, and Colonel Stewart the commander of the sharpshooters of the 49th Regiment who would man the tops. All of them had listened to Nelson's repeated exposition of the plan of battle, and though for most of those present it was the second or third time they had heard it the response was enthusiastic and the applause loud; it was not, thought Hardy, so much the brilliance of the plan (which was indeed simple enough) as the renewed contact with the fiery spirit that could infuse its flame into everyone round it. The wall of Danish ships and batteries, over 1,000 guns, had been prepared on the natural assumption that an attacking fleet would approach from the northern end of the King's Channel, the normal and safe route by which large vessels entered Copenhagen harbour. It was strongest at that northern end of the line, where the big guns of the Trekroner Fort defended the entrance. Nelson's light-draught ships, therefore, would enter the channel from the south, depending on a favourable wind, and anchor each in its appointed place to pound enemy ships and batteries into submission. Parker and his reserve would come in from the north when the supremacy of the King's Channel had been gained.

When the acclamation had abated Nelson sent his smiling glance round the eager faces of his captains. The contrast between the brilliance of the left eye and the dull opacity of the right was especially marked tonight.

"You all approve, I see," he said. "You look a trifle doubtful, Foley. You've something to suggest?"

"No, my lord, nothing," Foley said hastily.

"Good, good. Fremantle? Hardy?"

Hardy's honesty demanded that he should voice his criticism but he was reluctant to cool the general heat of enthusiasm. He sought for a way of blunting his shaft.

"The plan, my lord, has the Nelson touch about it, if I may say so," he said.

There was an instant buzz of appreciation and he could see that Nelson was delighted with his happy phrase.

"But there's a matter that needs care at the outset," he went on quickly. "The south-east wind we hope for will put the Middle Ground under our lee when we weigh tomorrow morning. You know, my lord, what leeway a 74 of light draught will make before she gets way on her. I'd suggest reaching well to the sou'-west—half-a-mile astern of the rearmost Danish ship—before bearing away up the King's Channel."

He could see the thin fingers of Nelson's left hand playing an impatient tattoo on the tablecloth before he had finished speaking. There were signs of impatience among the assembled captains, too; the speaker had no ship under his command in this operation and the fact tended to lessen the force of his argument.

"Captain Hardy forgets that we have pilots with us," Nelson said, frowning slightly, "north-country skippers who have traded to Copenhagen all their lives." His brow cleared and he nodded, smiling, at Hardy. "Never fear, Hardy, I shall weather every shoal. And then—" he stood up, glass in hand— "it's all over with the Danes. Gentlemen, a final toast—to a fair wind and victory!"

There was nothing in the words. It was the way he spoke them, the thrill of trumpets in the high thin voice. The captains, on their feet with glasses raised, echoed the toast as if it was a cheer, while the small figure in their midst (he looked like a child among them) grinned delightedly. Despite his doubts, Hardy drank the toast as enthusiastically as any man there; oddly enough, he could not now imagine any result but victory where Nelson led.

Graves and Riou went off with the Admiral to his cabin for further discussion, and the others dispersed. Hardy, following *Elephant*'s captain out onto the dark quarterdeck, laid a hand on his arm.

"There's a few things I'd like to borrow for an hour, Foley," he said in a low voice. "A boat and a boat's crew—"

"And a sounding-pole," Foley cut in, in the same tone. "It was in my mind too. All very well for his lordship to rely on these pilots, but I've heard them talking. They don't know this end of the channel and they'll refuse to take the responsibility of piloting the squadron. I'll give orders for your needs at once."

"Thank you, sir. And better muffle the oars."

An hour later Captain Hardy and his boat were two miles

from the squadron's flagship. The pale radiance from a cloudy night sky showed the ugly shape of a floating battery, the southernmost end of the Danish line, a pistol-shot away across the slow-heaving water. The thirty-foot pole rose and sank soundlessly in Hardy's big hands; he was handling it himself to save the necessity for uttering a word. Up came the pole, vertical and dripping. When its base was clear of the water its top, discernible against the sky, waggled with a circular motion. Obediently the men at the oars, using the utmost care, paddled the boat round, holding her steady when the pole ceased its waggling. At a gesture of the captain's free hand they urged her gently forward, the oars almost noiseless in their mufflings of sacking. Erect in the sternsheets with a knee against the tiller, Hardy could get a line-of-bearing using the black mass of the end battery and the just-visible tower of the Christiansborg castle; distance he could only judge by the boat's speed, but in that he had twenty years of experience. They were well beyond earshot of the battery when he checked the boat's progress with a word and began again to sound with the pole, groping along the same line until he found the rapid shallowing that betokened the edge of the Middle Ground. For another hour he sounded along the verge of the shoal, making slowly back to where the squadron lay dark and silent at anchor.

When he came on board *Elephant*, wet and chilled by the unavoidable drippings from the pole, he had gained a rough idea of the conformation of shallows and channel at the tip of the Middle Ground, but no more than that. Whether or not it would be of service was doubtful.

3

At half-past nine on the morning of April 2nd Captain Hardy stood on *Elephant*'s quarterdeck, in the most inconspicuous place he could find and feeling a trifle lost with no duties assigned to him. In a hurried aside Foley had asked him to take charge if he should be killed or wounded but that was all. He watched the bustle as the flagship's anchor was hove in sight, as the larboard upper-deck guns were loaded and run out, as red-coated soldiers of the 49th clambered to the fighting-tops. Then he turned his full attention to the progress of the ships ahead in the line, now getting under way with their topsails flapping and filling.

There had been an even chance of a south-easterly wind this morning and the chance had come off, though it was only the lightest of breezes. Under the grey overcast the ruffled water stretching away to the waiting rank of Danish ships showed a dull green, and behind the long wall of vessels the buildings and spires of Copenhagen spread darkly along the low coast. *Edgar*, leading the line, was moving slowly towards the invisible channel; she would just, Hardy thought, clear the tip of the Middle Ground. He knew that Foley's prophecy had come true and that every pilot had refused to take the leading ship in. He could see the lead going as *Edgar* moved steadily on with *Agamemnon* following her and *Isis* coming third. *Glatton, Ardent, Bellona*, and now it was *Elephant*'s turn to brace her topsails and gather way. A slow business, thought Hardy, slower than St Vincent or the Nile; it would be an hour before *Edgar* came within range of the floating battery he had come so close to last night. The ship was almost silent. The chant of the leadsmen in the chains sounded like the responses in a cathedral service, giving this prelude to slaughter the air of a religious procession. The upper-deck gun crews squatted motionless under the hammock-nettings beside their charges, the soldiers in the tops were invisible and inaudible. Nelson and Foley, walking to and fro a few yards from Hardy's position by the lee rail, were the only persons moving on the quarterdeck.

Beneath the big cocked hat (his hats were always too big for him) Nelson's pale face was animated and eager as he talked to the captain. The eyes of the men waiting by the guns followed him as he passed; the legendary figure, the shrimp of a man in his coat with the three stars and the empty sleeve, was something more to them than a talisman—almost a god, Hardy realised. Unlike King George and the Lords of the Admiralty, they felt increased respect and affection for a god with feet of clay, who had left a fancy-woman behind in London.

An urgent hail from the lieutenant in charge of the for'ard guns drew the attention of the quarterdeck to *Agamemnon*, ahead in the line. The 64, Nelson's old command, had failed to weather the tip of the Middle Ground and had run on the shoal. In these nearly tideless waters there was no hope of getting her off without prolonged towing and kedging, and the Admiral, showing signs of agitation, ordered *Polyphemus* signalled to take her place. Eleven ships were left to attack the score of floating gun-platforms awaiting them.

The head of the line was safely round the shoal and steering north-north-west, *Edgar* slowly closing the battery at the end of the Danish rank. *Crash!* went the Danish guns as she came within range. Hardy took his watch from his fob : twenty minutes to eleven. *Edgar* held on without replying, to withstand a second storm of shot from the next floating battery before anchoring by the stern opposite a Danish battleship, the third in the rank. The thunder of the opposing broadsides roared and great dun-coloured clouds of smoke billowed and spread, augmented as *Polyphemus* and *Isis* encountered the fire of the batteries. By now Hardy was standing on the rail, steadying himself with a hand on the mizen shrouds while he peered anxiously ahead. This was the crucial point they were coming to now, the scene of his expedition of last night, the place where the weakness in Nelson's plan could lead to disaster.

Though a line of moored ships was being attacked by a line of ships under sail, as at the Nile, there was here no possibility of attack from both sides. The British line had perforce to

152

take up battle stations opposite the starboard side of the Danes and employ only their own larboard guns; and since, obviously, it was folly for the leading British ships to run the gauntlet of the whole enemy rank in order to anchor opposite the ships at the head of it, they would anchor in succession starting at the rear end of the rank. Each vessel thus had to pass her immediate leader when that leader anchored. She could not pass to larboard, between two enemies busily hurling shot at each other, therefore she must pass to starboard, between her next-ahead and the unseen edge of the Middle Ground shoal. Hardy could make only a rough estimate of the width of the channel and their position in it, but he knew how steep-to was the edge of the shoal. Beyond *Bellona*, who was just ahead of *Elephant*, he made out two ships—*Glatton* and *Ardent*, they would be—passing from sight into the battle-cloud out of which, increasing every minute, came the din of the guns.

"Well, Hardy, no manœuvring here." Nelson had crossed the deck to speak to him. "Just downright fighting."

The rearmost floating battery, which they were passing, opened fire as he stopped speaking and the deck shuddered to the impact of shot. *Elephant*'s guns remained silent.

"Yes, my lord," said Hardy; he touched his hat in salute but did not descend from his observation-post.

Bellona was entering the smoke-cloud. Over to larboard loomed the British ships already engaged with the enemy. Now *Elephant* was into the smoke and it was next to impossible to gauge position in relation to the Danish line.

"*Bellona*'s anchoring, I fancy," said the Admiral, peering from the rail beside him.

The ship ahead appeared to have stopped. *Elephant* was overhauling her, her bows beginning to swing to starboard as Captain Foley prepared to pass her. Hardy's narrowed gaze caught the tilt of *Bellona*'s masts, the flutter of her topsails. He shouted with the full force of his lungs.

"Starboard your helm, Foley! Starboard—helm!"

Foley snapped the order at his quartermasters without hesitation. The wheel spun to starboard and *Elephant*'s bows swung slowly round to larboard, clearing *Bellona*'s stern by a narrow margin. As they sheered past her someone shouted from her deck.

"We're aground!"

Two ships out of it. Nelson had summoned a signal lieutenant and was gesticulating with his one arm as he gave his orders. Hardy strode to the after-rail to stare at the grounded ship as she fell astern. *Defiance*, next in line, saw the danger and passed to larboard; but as he watched he saw the ship astern of her—*Russell*, last but one of the British line—steer to starboard according to her orders and shudder to a stop almost alongside *Bellona*. Nine were left of the twelve British ships.

But now the men of the cable-party came racing aft and *Elephant*'s stern anchor splashed down. Hardy had a brief glimpse of the big Danish ship a cable-length away on the larboard beam—the flagship *Dannebrog*—before she disappeared behind the smoke of her first broadside. The thirty-six guns of *Elephant*'s larboard broadside roared out a few seconds later. After that, the British flagship became a small and separate world of noise and death, ringed by the drifting swathes of acrid-smelling smoke; a world wherein eight hundred men toiled and agonised with the sole object of battering another ship and other men into final ruin. Two thousand great oak-trees, a golden wealth of craftsmanship and ingenuity, long years of training and discipline, had forged this composite weapon with no other object in view. Victory in a righteous cause was its only justification.

Thoughts such as these would not have passed through Hardy's mind but for his unprecedented lack of occupation. He had no doubt of victory, even though the opening phase of the action had been disastrous for the British; he had no doubt of the righteousness of his cause, either. It did not occur to him to ask whether a neutral nation had not a right to decide where its goods should be sold, for he believed that no nation could be neutral in the face of France's boast that she would conquer the world. Nor had he suddenly reversed his firm conviction that it was right and proper for men to fight and die in battle. It was the fact that he had no responsibility, no ship or guns or men to command, that had allowed his reflections to become (as he told himself) so damned nonsensical. He found himself intensely disliking his rôle of onlooker; it weakened those protective mental walls with which he was accustomed to surround himself during an action. The deafening uproar of cannon-fire numbed his brain, the shriek of a ball whistling close overhead made him jump, and he came within an ace of vomiting when one of the hands manning the quarterdeck carronades was hurled back and fell almost at his feet with a mash of red-and-grey pudding where his head should have been. He made himself step forward, shouting to one of the cockpit duty-men to take the corpse away; and felt a little better.

His period of numbed inaction must have been considerable, he realised. When *Elephant*'s first broadside was fired the Admiral had been walking the starboard side of the quarterdeck with Captain Foley, whereas now it was Colonel Stewart who paced with him. As the two turned near the foot of the mast a shot struck it, showering them with splinters.

"All right, my lord?" Hardy heard the Colonel say anxiously.

"Right as a trivet, Colonel." Nelson raised his voice to a screech, so as to be heard above the din. "It's warm work—but mind you, I wouldn't be elsewhere for thousands."

They resumed their pacing. Somehow that high-pitched voice roused Hardy from the curious lethargy that had gripped him, and he began to look critically about him. From the noise of gunnery to northward that portion of the Danish line was in fierce action, so *Defiance*, *Ganges* and *Monarch* must have passed the flagship to gain their battle stations. With only nine ships, though, there would be no vessels to engage the Trekroner Fort. Foley, standing by the wheel, caught his eye and Hardy crossed the deck to him, dodging aside from a brace of seamen who were carrying a man whose leg had been taken off at the knee.

"You'd oblige me, Captain Hardy," said Foley, "if you'd visit the maindeck for me. I've had no report from Mr Duff for the past half-hour and I don't want to leave the quarterdeck."

Glad of occupation of any sort, Hardy went down into the inferno of the maindeck, where amid the yells and clatter and ear-splitting explosions he ascertained that Lieutenant Duff had been severely wounded—a splinter through the groin— and taken to the surgeons; it was to be presumed that if any messenger had been sent to the captain he had been killed or wounded on the way. Hardy found a begrimed midshipman and dispatched him to the quarterdeck to tell Foley what had happened and that he, Hardy, would take charge of the maindeck guns, all of which were still in action. And for the next forty-five minutes he was content, though the *Dannebrog*'s guns smashed two mighty gaps in the maindeck timbers and a ball that entered through a gunport made red ruin among the crew of a 16-pounder.

Stalking up and down the line of leaping, thundering guns, stopping for a curt word of commendation or reproof for the sweating gunners, he was momentarily back on the tilted maindeck of *Minerve*, five years ago. He had met Nelson for the first time, he remembered, five days before that running fight with *Sabina*. He had thought him imprudent, vain, needing to be looked after; and he had disliked him. Now, he thought no differently of him but (he had to admit it) he had more affection for Nelson than for any other human being. The little man up there on the quarterdeck, strutting to and fro with bullets and splinters flying round him, was almost like a part of himself—so much so, indeed, that the stoic unconcern under which Hardy crushed his emotions during an action seemed to have extended itself to cover Nelson as well, for he felt no anxiety for the Admiral's safety. Nevertheless, when he came on deck again he let out an unconscious sigh of relief at the sight of Nelson alive and unhurt.

The order to cease fire had taken Hardy by surprise. With even more surprise he noted, as he came up the ladder to the quarterdeck, that his watch marked the time as half-past two. Through the clearing drifts of smoke he saw the gunners resting wearily beside the larboard carronades, dead and wounded men being carried below, a splintered gap in the rail —already a working-party was clearing the clutter of broken wood and torn hammocks. Across the water the *Dannebrog* was on fire and the grey waves were littered with spars and timber, men swimming or floating motionless, boats pulling in all directions. Southward down the line from *Elephant* the gunfire had ceased, though to northward, towards the Trekroner Fort, ships were still in action. Nelson was standing by the casing of the rudder-head, using the casing as a desk while Foley's purser, Wallis, steadied the paper he was writing on. With them was Colonel Stewart, Fremantle of the *Ganges*, and a young captain who was unknown to Hardy.

"I'll have your opinion on that, Fremantle," Nelson said briskly, handing the paper to him. "Yours also, Hardy," he added as Hardy approached.

The spidery writing was plain enough :

"To the Brothers of Englishmen, the Danes.
Lord Nelson has directions to spare Denmark when no longer resisting; but if the firing is continued on the part of Denmark Lord Nelson will be obliged to set on fire all the Floating-batteries he has taken, without having the power of saving the brave Danes who have defended them.
Dated on board His Britannic Majesty's ship Elephant, *Copenhagen Roads, April 2nd, 1801."*

It was signed: *"Nelson and Brontë, Vice-Admiral, under the command of Admiral Sir Hyde Parker."*

"Excellent, my lord," Fremantle said, and Hardy grunted assent. "But the day's ours and Sir Hyde's squadron is in sight. We could finish the Danes, once and for all."

"I don't propose to finish them, Fremantle," Nelson said testily. "My task was to prevent their ships uniting with the Russian fleet. This letter begins another task, and a damned difficult one. I've to turn enemies into friends."

Captain Foley hurried up to the group at the rudder-head. "The boat's alongside, my lord. Flag-of-truce rigged in the sternsheets."

"Very well, Foley. Captain Thesiger, you'll take the boat to the quays and find the Prince Regent. Colonel Stewart will go with you—"

He walked with the two officers towards the rail.

"Well, Hardy, that'll be the end of it, if the Danes can see sense," Foley said with relief. "Can't say I'm sorry—I've lost at least sixty killed and twice that wounded. I may as well set my ship in order, and that'll be no easy job."

"I'll help, if I may."

"Thank you. Did you know Admiral Parker signalled us an hour ago? Number Thirty-nine was what he hoisted."

"Leave off action?" Hardy said incredulously.

"Just that. I suppose he'd made out we'd only nine ships in the line." Foley chuckled. "*London* was hull-up from the deck here, so Lord Nelson borrowed my glass to see for himself. 'You know, Foley,' says he with that droll glance of his, 'I've only one eye—I've a right to be blind sometimes.' Then he puts the glass to his eye—his dead eye, you understand. 'No, I'm damned if I can see the signal,' he says. 'Mind you keep Number Sixteen flying, Foley,' which is for close action, as you know. Oh, he's a great man, is our Nel."

"He's a great admiral," Hardy said slowly. "That's sure.

He'll be a great man if he can make friends of the Danes after this."

He pointed across the broken rail. The Danish flagship was a mass of leaping flames. Her cables had burned through and she was drifting northward along the front of the Danish line, creating havoc and consternation as she went. From her open ports such men as were still alive threw themselves into the water, where the boats of both British and Danes sheered as close as they dared to the blazing ship to pick them up. A short time later, having grounded, *Dannebrog* blew up with heavy loss of life. But by then all guns had ceased to fire and the Battle of Copenhagen was over.

4

Overhead the sky was pale-blue and cloudless. A sea as smooth as blue glass stretched to the horizon, and the sun's heat raised a diminishing quiver of steam from the newly-scrubbed deck. The Baltic Sea had lost all its winter bleakness in the two months that had passed since the Battle of Copenhagen. Captain Hardy, eyeing *St George*'s transformed quarterdeck with a critical gaze, felt the hot rays on the shoulders of his best uniform coat and was reminded of the Mediterranean.

"Strings of bunting from the canopy to the rail?" he said doubtfully. "Bunches of ribands on its for'ard end, maybe? What's your opinion, Mr Lyne?"

"Bunting, sir—yes," said the first lieutenant with decision. "Ribands—no. Too much like frippery."

"Very well. Rouse out the spare signal-flags."

Mr Lyne departed, calling a bosun's mate from his task of draping a Royal Standard artistically over the seat and back of a large chair. Captain Hardy took a turn on the quarterdeck, selecting a walk that did not interfere with a party of hands under Mr Fere the fourth lieutenant, who were measuring distances on the planking with a lead-line and marking them with chalk.

The peaceful scene around him reflected the real peace that had settled upon this northern sea and its surrounding countries. For the peace with Denmark at the end of April Nelson was personally, almost solely, responsible; that much Hardy had realised from what he had heard, for he had not attended the Admiral on those diplomatic visits to Copenhagen. He knew that Nelson had been quite alone in the first interview with the Prince Regent of Denmark and his counsellors, which had resulted in the initial armistice; and that the final settlement, eminently satisfactory to Britain, had been won by Nelson's refusal to show either enmity or weakness when confronted with unreasonable Danish demands. From several Danes (and a great many had come on board *St George* in the course of the negotiations) he had learned of the remarkable impression Nelson's personality had made in Copenhagen, so that he had actually been cheered in the streets; and on the day before the squadron sailed he had been able to confirm this himself. Hardy was no hand at writing letters, but he had lately corresponded at long intervals with John Manfield, his sister's husband. In a letter to John he confessed—perhaps unconsciously—the completeness of his devotion. *"The more I see of his Ldship the more I must admire him, for on this occasion his Political management was if possible greater than his bravery,"* he wrote; and: *"His Ldship and myself was on shore y'day, when extraordinary to be told, he was received with as much acclamation as when we went to Lord Mare's Show."*

And the subsequent weeks of cruising up the Baltic had shown that the Armed League was dissolved. The news of the assassination of the Tsar of Russia was succeeded by friendly approaches by the new Tsar, his son. The Swedes, with their eight ships of the line, would not move without Russia and

Denmark. The British Fleet was to remain in the Baltic until August; and here was, for Captain Hardy, the fly in the ointment. For Nelson, Viscount Nelson as he was now, was by his own request going home to England in the frigate *Aeolus*, his place being taken by Admiral Pole. As for Sir Hyde Parker, he had been recalled to England in May, and Hardy had been as pleased as his Admiral when Nelson had been given the command. And now he was to stay and Nelson was to go. Today's ceremony would be Nelson's last act as commander of the Channel Fleet.

The sloop from England that had brought the news of Lord Nelson's viscountcy had also brought him instructions from King George. Rear-Admiral Graves had been awarded the Order of the Bath and Vice-Admiral Lord Nelson was to invest him with it. Remembrance of that reminded Captain Hardy that there was little time left before the ceremony was due to begin. He went below for his sword.

Half-an-hour later *St George*'s quarterdeck was a stratum of brilliant colours raised between blue sea and blue sky. Ranked on larboard and starboard sides were the red coats of the marines and the soldiers of the 49th regiment; the blue and white and gold of a score of naval captains made the third side of a hollow square, and the chair and canopy (with Lyne's bunting fluttering on either hand) stood in the fourth side. Nelson, stepping from beside the simulated throne, laid his sword on the shoulder of the kneeling Graves, dubbing him Sir Thomas, and as he placed the red ribbon over the shoulder of the new Companion of the Bath the for'ard guns of the flagship fired a salute. Hardy, watchful in the background, was perhaps the only man present who knew that the Admiral's firm step and erect bearing concealed a state approaching physical and nervous exhaustion. It was as well that he was going home, he reflected; heroes were not immortal, and this one could ill be spared when there were great sea-fights still to come.

SIX

1

Pitt was out and Addington was in. The unfaltering voice so resolute for war had given place to the uncertain pronouncements of a mere politician. Captain Hardy, stolidly pursuing the uneventful routine of shipboard, scanned the letters and newspapers brought out to the Baltic fleet and shook his head over them. Their tone reflected the growing inclination towards the consideration, at least, of peace terms with France, and some journalists produced plausible reasons. Britain was again mistress of the seas, but Bonaparte was still master of Europe; the vast fleets of the Continental powers were held inactive by the British blockade, but their armies were far too strong to be challenged in Europe by a British army unaided. It was stalemate, and the only way out was a negotiated peace. But Captain Hardy still shook his head.

When the *St George* returned to Yarmouth in September he was appointed to command the *Isis*, 74, one of the now famous nine ships that had withstood the battering of the Danish guns. *Isis* was refitting in Portsmouth dockyard, a long job by reason of her ruinous state. In the intervals of wrestling with dilatory dockyard officials Hardy heard news of Nelson that worried and angered him. Immediately on his return from the Baltic, the nation's hero (as he now was in very truth) had been appointed by Admiralty to command the flotilla of small ships that defended Thames mouth and the Kent coast against the threatened French invasion. This, a command that could have been given to any one of a score of junior sea-officers, was particularly unsuited to an ailing one-armed man of middle age who needed to recuperate after the rigours of the Baltic campaign. From Captain Parker, a young officer invalided ashore from the flotilla, Hardy learned how Nelson, with his admiral's flag hoisted in a very small frigate, was enduring the worst autumn weather for years; how he was daily racked with seasickness and suffered perpetual colds and fevers; how his application to be relieved of his command had been flatly refused. Despite this he had devised a number of raids on the French coast, most of which had been unsuccessful. It was ridiculous, said Parker, to employ a Vice-Admiral, who had led battle fleets to victory, in affairs that could be better managed by a lieutenant of half his age—with two good arms. What the devil did their Lordships think they were about?

Captain Hardy suspected what they were about. He paid a visit to the Admiralty and was granted an interview with Sir Thomas Troubridge, now First Sea Lord. Troubridge received him with cool politeness in a large room of oak panelling and mahogany furniture and dismissed four secretaries before waving his visitor to a seat. His round face had lost in pleasantness what it had gained in dignity since they had first met five years ago, and his brown eyes were no longer candid.

"I suppose your business concerns *Isis*, Captain Hardy?" he said with a trace of impatience.

"My business, Sir Thomas," Hardy began; and checked himself. "You might say it's none of my business," he added slowly. "That depends whether I'm speaking to the First Sea Lord or to Tom Troubridge of the *Culloden*."

Troubridge frowned and shifted in his chair. "You're at liberty to speak plainly to me, Hardy. But I warn you, I can only hear you as a loyal servant of Admiralty."

"H'm." Hardy tugged at his ear. "Well, then, I'd like to know this. Why was Vice-Admiral Lord Nelson given this piddling flotilla command that's like to be his death, when what he needed was to be ordered into hospital for a month?"

"By God!" the First Sea Lord exploded, reddening angrily. "You were damned right when you said it was none of your business. But I'll answer you. If Nelson had been ordered to hospital, as you suggest, d'ye think he'd have gone there? No —he'd have been off for a spell of hugger-mugger with Emma Hamilton, and you know it."

"Ah," Hardy said softly. "So as soon as Lord Nelson comes back from Copenhagen he's packed off into the first command that offers, no matter what—to keep him away from Lady Hamilton. Is that right?"

"And what if it is? I'm in full agreement with Lord St Vincent that the Hamilton affair must be curbed somehow, and so must Nelson. The man thinks that because he's a fine sea-officer, which nobody denies, he can do what he likes."

"With his private life, Sir Thomas, he can, surely."

"No he can't!" Troubridge flashed. "He's the hero of the mob, a public figure, a pillar of the Government—and a kind of symbol of the Navy, what's more. Nelson pockets all that and—and won't or can't see where his responsibility lies. Look at him now!" The First Sea Lord was lashing himself into a fury. "Casts off his wife, who's a good and faithful woman. Buys this Merton Place in Surrey, puts Hamilton and Hamilton's wife in it, pays for Sir William's board and lodging so that he and Emma can have a bed to themselves. Everyone knows it. The French newspapers gloat over it. And I'm told he's begotten a child on her already."

"You know that?" Hardy said sharply.

Troubridge stiffened and lowered his gaze. "Lord St Vincent has received reliable information."

"Your Lordships have set spies on him, then?"

The rasp in Hardy's tone seemed to recall Troubridge's chilly dignity. He mastered his anger and spoke sharply.

"You presume too far, Captain Hardy, on our old acquaintance." He stood up. "This interview is at an end."

Hardy rose slowly to his feet. "I'll presume to remind you, Sir Thomas, of what you once told me concerning Lord Nelson. There's no living man, you said, better fitted to command a British fleet against the enemy. That's still true. It's Admiralty's business to keep it true. And scrounch me if I see how parting him from Emma Hamilton will serve anyone but Bonaparte!"

He stalked from the room without waiting for an answer. His feelings, as he returned the salutes of the sentries at Whitehall gates, held more than a trace of sorrow: he had lost Troubridge's friendship, and he was a man who did not make friends easily. But he had no regrets for speaking his mind. It was odd, he reflected, that when Troubridge had spoken those words it had been Troubridge who defended Nelson, Hardy who was reluctant to think well of him. Five years had reversed their positions. Whether his blundering intervention would do anything to help Nelson out of his present painful servitude was very doubtful; but it would certainly do Captain Hardy no good in his relations with Their Lordships and he could expect some manifestation of their disfavour. His expectation was soon justified.

In March of 1802, a month after that interview with the First Sea Lord, peace was signed. Mr Addington called it the Peace of Amiens, the London wits called it "the peace that passeth understanding". Captain Hardy called it nonsensical. It was loudly welcomed by a war-weary nation, but he was one of many who discerned that there could never be peace between a free country and a dictator bent on world domination. And Bonaparte was now a dictator, Consul of France for life and signing himself royally "Napoleon" or with a simple initial. For the moment, however, the Peace was a fact, accepted as permanent in Britain though by no means so in France. Earl St Vincent, a niggard in old age, began his stringent reduction of naval ships and supplies. *Isis*, newly refitted, was ordered to pay off and her captain to relinquish his command without further appointment. Once again Hardy was on half-pay, a captain without a ship.

And now the weeks passed slowly and sadly for him. He took up quarters in his old lodgings near Fladong's for a while, but "coffee-housing" in time of peace held out much less hope of finding employment than in time of war and he quickly wearied of gossiping and drinking with other shipless captains. A visit of courtesy to Number 54 St James's Street proved abortive; Lady Nelson, he learned, had accompanied the aged Rector of Burnham Thorpe to Bath. Hardy found himself relieved that he would not have to meet her. His sympathies had been honestly and freely given two years ago, but since then he had insensibly moved closer to Nelson, and his single-mindedness could not tolerate a divided loyalty. Fanny Nelson had right on her side and in their joint relation her husband was indubitably wrong; but Hardy now cared only for Horatio Nelson's happiness and well-being, and was anxious only lest the Admiral should miss the chance (which he still firmly believed would come) to prove himself the greatest sea-officer of the age.

He had few friends in London and no close ones, and their company did nothing to remove the unease he felt whenever he was long absent from the neighbourhood of the only man to whom he was sincerely attached. It was no fault of Nelson's that the absence was prolonged. As soon as the Peace released him from his command the Admiral had retired to his new property of Merton Place, there to set up as a country gentleman with Emma as Lady of the Manor while Sir William Hamilton, a complacent background, alternated between catching fish and quizzing antiquities. A letter had reached Hardy within a fortnight of Nelson's arrival at Merton, inviting his one-time flag-captain to come for an extended stay. Hardy had declined it on an invented excuse. He could not bring himself to endure Emma Hamilton as hostess even for the reward of being with Nelson.

Autumn came, and Hardy went home to Portisham. The shooting-parties quickly palled, and the society of his family —involved, as usual, in intricate warfare with relations— wearied him. Susan Manfield, he learned, was married and had left the district. He returned to London in December, and found awaiting him a letter from Nelson inviting—or rather commanding—him to dinner at Merton; the title-deed of Hardy's Sicilian estate, added the writer, was ready and must be handed over. Hardy remembered that Nelson had once said (jestingly, as he had thought at the time) that a hundred acres of his "Dukedom" at Brontë should be Hardy's. He did not want to accept the invitation but it was impossible to decline.

So he went to Merton, an hour's drive from London Bridge; a big country mansion with a stream wandering through its wooded grounds. To see Nelson's angular face light up with pleasure when he came in through the outer door, to feel the hard grip of the bony hand, made the first few minutes of his visit enjoyable. The rest he hated, for it blared forth as with discordant trumpets the aspect of Horatio Nelson which Hardy found utterly distasteful.

The whole house was like a temple to Nelson the god. Pictures of Nelson, of all sizes and sorts, covered the walls of every room and the sides of the great staircase. Relics of Nelson's ships, trophies of Nelson's victories, occupied every niche and corner. As if all these were not obvious enough Emma Hamilton had to point them out, each in turn, to the visitor. Lady Hamilton had become very fat; there was no other word for it. Hardy calculated mentally that with twenty inches of height less than himself her weight was about the same as his. She gave no sign that she remembered their bickerings at Naples three years ago. At dinner there were eight or nine other people; some relatives named Matcham, a Mr Davison and his lady, Sir William Hamilton looking venerable and abstracted, a squat and silent elderly woman called Mrs Cadogan who (he gathered) was Emma's mother. None of them seemed to perceive anything remarkable about Lady Hamilton's behaviour at table, so Hardy concluded that it was usual. She chanted, an unwearying priestess, a continual paean to Nelson. Every attempt at ordinary conversation was at once seized by her and turned to blatant flattery of the man at her side. She caressed him, stroked his hair or his hand, kissed him a dozen times before them all. And the hero accepted it with quiet enjoyment, precisely as he accepted the dishes that were set before him. Hardy, miserably embarrassed, did not enjoy the meal and was glad to get away at last with the promised title-deed in his pocket. And yet, as he clattered back along the dark road in his chaise, he had to admit himself satisfied on the most important point. Nelson was looking well and happy. If it was unpleasant to know that he thrived on the kind of treatment he was getting at Merton Place, it was better than worrying about a Nelson ill and neglected.

It was a lonely Christmas in London for Captain Hardy. Fladong's knew his occasional visits in the early weeks of 1803, but it was not until late February that he knew he was to be employed again. The post was a lowly one for a man who had commanded a flagship of 98 guns—the command of the Portsmouth guardship; but he accepted it without hesitation and betook himself on board the 32-gun frigate *Amphion*.

And slowly at first, but gathering swift momentum, came in those Spring months the rumour and then the certainty of war. Napoleon broke faith and with threats and bullying asserted his right to do so. The mask was flung aside. He would have nothing less than all Europe, and if Britain stood in his way he would sweep her out of it.

On a windy May morning a lugger brought a sealed package out to *Amphion*, at anchor in Spithead. From its contents Captain Hardy learned that he was to take command of His

Majesty's ship *Victory* of 100 guns, flagship of Vice-Admiral Lord Nelson, K.B., appointed to the Mediterranean Command.

2

Minerve was Hardy's first love; *Victory* was his last, where ships were concerned. He had never felt much affection for *Vanguard* or *Foudroyant*, and though long years afterwards he was to have a flagship of his own he was never as happy in her as he was in *Victory*.

She was twenty-seven years old when he took command, but during the Peace she had been given an extensive refit and had been partly rebuilt, her old-fashioned stern galleries being removed to give her the flat stern of more modern ships. Vice-Admiral Lord Nelson was as fond of her as his flag-captain and took some pains with her appearance. He had her sides painted with varnish-yellow and black bands between the three gun-decks; the port-lids were painted black, so that with the gunports closed the sides were chequered black-and-yellow. Her masts were yellow and the fighting-tops black. The sensation she caused when she joined the Mediterranean Fleet gave the Admiral unbounded delight and caused half-a-dozen captains to start painting their own ships *à la Nelson*.

And the long blockade began again. In the impregnable ports, under the guns of Brest and Rochefort and Toulon, the French battleships lay immobile, watched by the frigates of the British squadrons outside. If ever they put to sea they were to be attacked and defeated at all costs, but the essential thing was that they must not escape to threaten the British lifelines of commerce. The wealth of the City, the sinews of war, had its main source in the rich islands of the West Indies, and that convoy route above all must not be endangered. From Toulon, where a dozen French warships (two of them newly constructed) were known to be in harbour, an escaping fleet might also threaten Egypt and the riches of India; Napoleon was known to have designs in that direction. With nine battleships and eight frigates Nelson had to watch Toulon, guard Naples, and provide convoy escort for the British Mediterranean trade. Constant vigilance went side-by-side with the monotony of routine in that service, where for month after month the faint but ineradicable hope of action was deferred and officers and men lost heart for simple lack of anything to strike at.

As summer wore on into autumn with rumours and false alarms leading to nothing, Captain Hardy found another aspect of Nelson to admire—the foresight and skill that averted the dangers of slackness and mutiny. The Admiral devoted himself to the men under his command. He personally saw to it that their food was fresh and good and their clothing adequate; the peculations of a naval storekeeper, the question of supplying longer jerseys for topmen in winter, the ordering of oranges from Malta, all were dealt with by Nelson. Captains were advised to organise amateur theatricals among their crews (the Admiral loved to attend the performances) and the captains themselves dined regularly with Nelson on board *Victory*. Hardy, present and watchful at these dinner-parties, perceived and marvelled at what Troubridge had once called "Nelson's extraordinary power of infusing his own spirit into everyone round him".

Hardy himself was busy throughout the summer working to make *Victory* the efficient fighting ship his stern perfectionism required. He had nine hundred men to train, nine lieutenants to be taught his strict rules of discipline. In Quilliam, his first lieutenant, he had an invaluable assistant. Quilliam was lean and humorous, of a reflective turn of mind but swift and intelligent when action was required. He had a way, remarkable to the less imaginative Hardy, of seeing the odder side of naval matters. One winter day when the two were pacing the quarterdeck and talking, as usual, of their ship and her people, Hardy declared his satisfaction that every member of the crew was well enough trained to be called a British seaman.

"So a French seaman can be called a British seaman," Quilliam remarked.

"Eh?" Hardy was momentarily startled. "Oh—I take you. We've three Frenchmen in *Victory*'s crew, sure."

"Yes, sir," nodded the first lieutenant. "We've also Spaniards, Scandinavians, Negroes, Hindus, Germans, Italians, Portuguese, Kanakas, Swiss, Dutch, and Americans. Every man-jack of them is a British seaman."

"Every man-jack of them knows his duty, Mr Quilliam," Hardy said with a touch of asperity. "That's what matters in a British ship."

Christmas passed and the new year of 1804 began with week after week of storm in the Mediterranean. Blown off station more than once, forced sometimes to seek the shelter of Maddalena Bay on the Sardinian coast, the blockading squadron nevertheless fulfilled its task. Nelson, who had only once set foot on shore in nine months, succumbed to his old enemy seasickness, which allied itself with a chill. Dr Beatty, *Victory*'s surgeon, confided to her captain that a man so frail of body as the Admiral invited serious illness by being on deck in all weathers and taking far too little sleep. But Nelson, weak and wan, was himself again in a week and looking as eagerly as ever for some sign of the enemy's preparing to come out and fight.

"Fight he may," he told Hardy, "but if he does it will be hit-and-run, to get past us and away. Depend upon it, Bonaparte wants Monsieur Villeneuve for something big, and won't let him risk a hammering."

Spring and summer brought an alarm or two. An outburst of gunfire from Toulon one June night alerted the British ships, but it turned out to be a *feu-de-joie* in celebration of Napoleon's accession as Emperor of the French. Eight of the

Toulon ships made a sudden appearance a mile out of port and went through what was clearly a series of exercises. From a captured privateer schooner and a number of small merchant ships it was learned beyond doubt that there were eleven ships of the line and eighteen frigates ready for sea in Toulon harbour, and (with less certainty) that large numbers of troops were gathering at Toulon for embarkation. In late autumn came news that Spain, hitherto a dubious neutral, had declared war; her thirty-two ships of the line, now at the Emperor's service, were blockaded in Cadiz at once, but it was yet another strain on the divided squadrons of Britain. And once again Napoleon's Grand Army was practising embarkation on the Channel coast, preparing for that long-predicted time—only six hours was needed, said the Emperor—when the Combined Fleets of France and Spain should free the Straits from British warships and enable the invaders to cross.

But another Christmas came and passed without Villeneuve making a move. When he did make it, it seemed as though every ounce of good fortune was with him and against Nelson.

The watching frigates who brought the news that the French were at sea had lost them completely in thick weather; they could not report whether they were heading west or east. Nelson with his eleven ships searched the Mediterranean, his own charge, first. They were not there—this was not another attempted conquest of the East, then. Again perpetual head-winds he struggled back, to Gibraltar and a few doubtful scraps of information. The French had passed the Straits. They had united with six Spanish warships, making a Combined Fleet of eighteen of the line. But whether this fleet was bound for Ireland, or the Channel, or the West Indies, could only be answered by conjecture. Nelson decided on the last possibility. Resolving to take a Mediterranean Fleet to the West Indies meant the end of his career, the execration of the government, if he was wrong.

"To be burnt in effigy, or Westminster Abbey," he told Hardy. "Those are my alternatives."

Hardy said nothing. This variation on the Admiral's favourite saying in time of crisis reminded him of other occasions when Nelson's seeming rashness had brought him unscathed out of trouble. His faith in Nelson, now, was absolute. And all through the long chase that followed, while Nelson alternated between ecstasies of hope and agonies of despair, it was Hardy who stood unmoved by chances and changes, ready to comfort or restrain his volatile leader as occasion required, offering unobtrusive support at all times but counsel—unless he was specifically asked for it—never. He had come to know his part. Lacking the fire of genius that was Nelson's, he possessed the strength and stability that Nelson lacked and must do his clumsy best to share them with him.

So they stood on into the Trades and spoke two English merchant vessels who turned conjecture to certainty. The Combined Fleet, eighteen sail, was in the West Indies. At Barbados on the fourth of June the Governor of the Leeward Islands had heard that Villeneuve's ships had been seen heading south six days earlier, doubtless for Tobago or Trinidad. But Tobago and Trinidad had not seen them, and Grenada and Santa Lucia were safe. At Antigua Nelson's growing suspicion was confirmed: the French and Spanish admirals, learning that Nelson was at their heels, had abandoned their purpose of wresting the West Indies from the British and were on their way back to Europe. He sailed after them on June 13th.

Again it was a race, with Nelson in a fever of anxiety. The enemy had five days' start of him, and he could only guess what they would do when they reached the European coast. It was a not unlikely possibility that the opportunity of his absence would be seized, the allied fleets would break out and unite with Villeneuve, and that long-threatened thrust at England's heart from the Channel would be tried. He fulfilled his promise to "carry every rag, night and day," but could not overtake them. Finding no sign of them off Cape Spartel, he headed to join the Channel Fleet, and so had the news that the Combined Fleets, after an indecisive action with a blockading squadron under Sir Robert Calder, had won into the safe harbourage of Vigo. So *Victory* came back again to Portsmouth and Nelson to wild acclamation; he had saved the West Indies.

While the Admiral reported to the Commander-in-Chief and hastened on to Merton Place, Captain Hardy set about replenishing *Victory*'s stores and remedying the wear and tear of the flagship's two years at sea. He was not a man given to intuitions, nor had he Nelson's grasp of naval strategy; but it was plain even to him that the long chase to the West Indies and back had brought the struggle for sea-power to a head. The end of the chase had left the French and Spanish battle-fleets united and in a position to threaten the western approaches, the Channel, or a descent on Ireland. The threats could only become imminent danger when they had met and defeated the British fleet, but it was inconceivable that Napoleon should not seize the opportunity he had waited for so long and order them to sea. Hardy did not doubt that the Admiralty would muster their strongest ships for that crucial battle, and soon; still less did he doubt that Nelson would be given the command. He denied himself shore-leave and worked night and day to get *Victory* ready for the fight.

He was not mistaken. Twenty-five days after her arrival in Portsmouth from Antigua *Victory* sailed again, bound for a fleet rendezvous off Cadiz and carrying Vice-Admiral Lord Nelson to his greatest command.

3

The first sunlight of a dull day, October 21st, broke through the clouds an hour before noon. It glittered on the long Atlantic rollers off Cape Trafalgar and brought to life the colours of the great crescent of enemy ships two miles ahead—thirty-three French and Spanish ships, scarlet and yellow and black.

"That's a noble sight," said Captain Hardy. "It's a glorious sight, sure."

Admiral Lord Nelson, walking *Victory*'s quarterdeck with his flag-captain, halted as they turned and squinted up at his companion from under the green eyeshade he had taken to wearing over his left eye.

"Do you know, Hardy," he said half-humorously, "I've never heard you make a remark of that sort before."

"No, my lord?"

"No. But you're right, of course. They put a good face on it —and by God I'll give them such a dressing as they never had till now!"

The two resumed their walk; a restricted one, for the quarterdeck was crowded. The crews of the quarterdeck carronades, stripped to the waist, were standing-to on either hand, a single rank of marines was forming behind them, and on the lee side out of the Admiral's way a group of officers chattered in low voices as they watched the slow approach to battle. On the flagship's starboard hand the column of fifteen ships led by Collingwood's *Royal Sovereign* was gradually forging ahead of the eleven ships led by *Victory*. The breeze had weakened in the past hour and the two columns were advancing towards the Combined Fleets at a speed of less than two knots, under topsails and topgallants only.

"At this rate," muttered the Admiral, more to himself than to the captain, "we shall be under fire for twenty minutes before we can reply."

"What can't be cured must be endured," said Hardy; he remembered something that Mr Scott, the secretary, had suggested to him. "My lord, I'd advise a coat other than the one you're wearing. The sharpshooters in their tops will know where to aim."

175

Nelson glanced down at his left breast, where the stars of four orders of knighthood glittered.

"That may be," he said indifferently. "But it's too late to be shifting a coat."

They paced for a few moments in silence. Over to leeward the foremost of the black-and-yellow ships was little more than a mile from the rear ships of the enemy line. Hardy felt unusually elated, and was puzzled by his elation. It had already occurred to him that Nelson was displaying less emotion, less nervous excitement, than usual. If the idea hadn't been so nonsensical, a man might almost fancy that flag-captain and admiral had each absorbed something of the other's spirit in this hour before a great sea-fight. *If you and I were one man* —Nelson had said that once; at Naples, it had been, seven years ago.

"Hardy, I'm going to amuse the Fleet," the Admiral said, pausing in his walk. "Mr Pasco!" The signal lieutenant ran across to him. "I wish to say this to the Fleet, Mr Pasco— 'Nelson confides that every man will do his duty.' You'd best be quick about it, for I've one more signal to make."

"Aye aye, my lord." Pasco hesitated. "By your leave, my lord, 'expects' is in the signal book, and if we use that instead of 'confides' we can save seven hoists."

"Very well. And Mr Pasco—instead of 'Nelson' say 'England'."

Pasco touched his hat and dashed away. A minute later the hoist rose to *Victory*'s yardarm. Hardy watched the repeat hoists that rose, after the briefest of intervals, to the yardarms of all twenty-six British ships. Evidently the interpretation of the signal spread quickly to the waiting gunners and deckhands, for down the quartering wind came the sound of cheering. Nelson grinned and rubbed the armless "fin" that was pinned across his chest.

"Now make Number Sixteen, Mr Pasco, if you please."

The signal for Close Action duly flying, he went to the rail to stare across at the leeward column. *Royal Sovereign*, with the other fourteen ships close astern of each other, was almost within gunshot of the enemy line. Hardy had a momentary recollection of a dinner-party in *Victory*'s stern-cabin, and Nelson enthusiastically delivering himself of this plan of attack; the Fleet in two columns, one to break the enemy line between van and centre, the other to break it between rear and centre. And Collingwood, grim-faced and critical, demurring and being given his answer.

"What if the weather doesn't permit us, my lord?"

"My dear Coll, whatever happens no captain can do very wrong if he lays himself alongside an enemy ship."

Now Collingwood was almost into them. In another few minutes it would be *Victory*'s turn. The Nelson plan, reflected Hardy without emotion, meant inevitably that the leading ships of both columns must be subjected to the fire of half-a-dozen of the enemy before any aid could be given them.

"Coll's a gallant fellow, Hardy!" the Admiral exclaimed. "See how he carries his ship into action!"

Hard on his words came the boom of cannon-fire, the first shots of the battle. *Royal Sovereign*, with *Belleisle* and *Mars* on her heels, disappeared in a dilating cloud of smoke. Hardy glanced quickly aloft and along his upper deck. Quilliam, catching his eye from where he stood amidships, took off his hat and waved it. There was no need for further orders to the gundecks; from the lieutenants and midshipmen in charge to the smallest powder-monkey, everyone knew his duty there. He leaned from the rail to peer ahead.

"On this course, my lord, we shall break their line astern of a vessel wearing an admiral's flag."

"That will do very well."

"Steady as you go," Hardy growled at the helmsmen.

The roar of cannon was almost continuous to starboard as more of Collingwood's ships came into action. On *Victory*'s upper deck there was silence, while the faint breeze urged her slowly towards the uneven rank of enemy ships, themselves moving so slowly that they seemed to be waiting to be attacked. But it was *Victory* who had to wait, unable to bring a gun to bear as the first shots crashed into her. Long-range shots at first, passing overhead or falling alongside. Then a broadside from the French flagship, aimed high in the French fashion to disable masts and spars. A score of holes appeared in the sails, and Hardy saw the top third of the mizen topmast splinter and fall. Five minutes gone, he thought; if Nelson's estimate was right, and it probably was, there was another quarter-of-an-hour to endure—and the worst to come—before his guns could make reply.

Now the great hulls of enemy vessels could be seen close ahead on either bow. And here came the broadsides, one after another in close succession; the raking fire of six or seven ships. *Victory* shuddered and crept on, with white splinters flying from her rail and half-a-dozen men, seamen and marines, writhing or motionless on her deck. The Admiral's secretary was at Hardy's elbow, stammering out a request, something about his master's coat.

"He'll listen to you, sir. He must change it—"

There was a whistle and a thud. The secretary was a bundle of bloody rags under the quarterdeck rail. Again and again crashed the broadsides while the British gunners crouched inactive beside their weapons and their ship moved almost imperceptibly nearer to the French flagship. A tremendous impact shook the deck, and where an instant before the two quartermasters had been standing at the wheel there was now a splintered ruin draped with torn bodies streaming blood.

"Mr Quilliam!" Hardy's enormous voice topped the thunder of the cannonade. "Man the relieving-tackles below. Mr Atkinson!" The master came running aft. "You'll repeat my steering-orders."

Victory would have to be steered by means of the tiller in the gunroom two decks below the quarterdeck. Hardy took a quick glance ahead. Three minutes, perhaps, still to go. He turned to find the Admiral at his side.

"We'll walk, Hardy, if you please."

They began to pace solemnly to and fro, shaping their walk to avoid a pool of blood and halting once while a wounded marine was carried across the deck on his way to the cockpit. The din of enemy guns made conversation nearly impossible. A ball, smashing through the hammock-nettings and ricocheting off the forebrace bitts, enveloped the two men in a venomous spray of jagged splinters. They both halted and turned inwards to look each other up and down. Hardy shook his head with a smile and pointed to his left shoe, from which a flying splinter had torn the silver buckle. Nelson returned the smile.

"This is too warm work to last," he screeched above the uproar. "And yet I never saw guncrews cooler than our men, Hardy. They won't have to wait much longer, though."

"No longer," Hardy said. "Mr Atkinson! Larboard your helm!"

Victory came slowly round to starboard, crossing astern of the French flagship. And now, for the first time, her guns spoke, a double-shotted broadside that ripped through the Frenchman's stern windows and shattered her after-works to smithereens. Beyond her an 80-gun ship opened fire, and to starboard a French two-decker, the *Redoutable*, was so close that collision was inevitable. Through the narrow gap between the ships to larboard loomed an immense vessel painted vermilion and white, that same *Santissima Trinidada* of 136 guns whose fire had almost annihilated the *Captain* at the Battle of St Vincent. With these four vessels *Victory* now engaged in murderous duel, one against four, her 100 guns firing as fast as they could load. In the first few minutes she collided with *Redoutable* and though she fell away at the rebound her yardarm remained caught in the Frenchman's rigging. Locked in a death-grip, the two ships pounded ceaselessly at each other's sides.

Admiral Lord Nelson and Captain Hardy continued to pace up and down together through the swirling cannon-smoke, the acrid smell of burnt powder in their nostrils. Through a gap in the smoke Hardy caught sight of *Redoutable*'s mizen top, with the French marksmen firing from it; because of the two-decker's lesser height they were not far above *Victory*'s quarter-deck and less than fifty feet away. He observed this as he and Nelson made the turn at the limit of their walking-space, and he had taken three steps before he noticed that he was walking alone.

He swung round. Nelson was on his knees, supporting himself on his left arm. The arm gave way and he collapsed as Hardy reached him and knelt beside him. There was a little smile on his thin face.

"They've done for me at last, Hardy."

"No, my lord—no."

"Yes. My backbone is shot through."

Hardy winced as if he himself had been hit. He stood up quickly and looked round for help. Adair, captain of marines, came running with two seamen and at the same moment the third lieutenant, King, dashed across the littered deck.

"Boarding-party mustering on the Frenchman, sir," King panted. "On the foredeck yonder—" He broke off as he saw the Admiral. "My God! Is he—"

"Very well, Mr King," Hardy said loudly.

The seamen were lifting Nelson, who seemed to have lost consciousness. Hardy had taken a large handkerchief from his pocket and now he placed it so as to conceal Nelson's face and breast. The seamen began to shuffle towards the ladder. He turned his back on them and shouted above the uproar.

"Hands to repel boarders! For'ard, men—starboard side! Mr Adair, get your men for'ard, if you please, and don't wait to form them."

He ran up to the poop, kicking aside the headless body of

a marine so that he could get to the rail, and tried to see through the all-enveloping smoke. A musket-bullet buried itself in the wood of the rail three inches from his hand, another sang past his ear. Below him in the gulf between the two ships flame and smoke spurted from the battered hulls; but few of *Redoutable*'s guns were firing now. For'ard along his own deck there was nothing to be seen for smoke, but a roar of yells and cheering told of the hand-to-hand struggle going on there. Other cheers came distantly between the thundering broadsides; *Téméraire* and *Neptune* and *Conqueror* were into the line now and *Victory* was no longer alone. But close on the larboard bow loomed the dark flank of another Frenchman moving to the attack. The long yellow flames of her broadside stabbed through the smoke simultaneously with the thunder of the British flagship's larboard guns. The deck reeled under Hardy as he sprang down to the quarterdeck—to be besieged instantly by officers and petty officers with reports and demands. The boarders had been driven back but Captain Adair was killed; there were no gunners left alive at number eight gun upper deck; *Victory* was holed on the waterline but making little water as yet; fifty killed and wounded so far, at a guess.

He was dealing with all these in turn when a roar of cheering and the cessation of firing from the starboard guns betokened *Redoutable*'s surrender. Another ten minutes, and the ship on *Victory*'s other flank had been battered into silence. In the temporary lull the smoke drifted clear and Hardy, sending a man to the masthead, could look around him. The battle had become an affair of separated groups each locked in conflict, but even from the deck it could be seen that many French ships had struck. To northward, slowly bearing down on *Victory*, were five ships of the enemy's van who had so far been unable to take part in the fighting. He ordered a signal made, and having received the report of the seaman he had sent to the masthead went below, down the ladders sticky with blood to the lantern-lit shambles of the orlop deck.

A medley of groans, cries, half-stifled oaths and the sharp commands of the surgeon and his mates greeted him as he stooped his way along. The stench of blood and vomit was almost intolerable. In a cavern-like corner at the end of the orlop Nelson lay, attended by four or five men. They had got his coat off and ripped the shirt to expose his left shoulder, where the musket-ball had entered, and Dr Scott, *Victory*'s chaplain was holding a bloodstained cloth over the wound. Burke the purser crouched at the Admiral's side supporting the pillows which propped him in a position half sitting and half reclining. The yellow lantern-light did not reach the faces of the others but Hardy thought they were Nelson's valet and his steward. Behind them he could see Smith, the assistant surgeon, working on an ugly head-wound (his patient, he noted, was Bligh, fifth lieutenant) but there was no sign of the man he was most anxious to talk to.

Nelson's eyes were closed, his deeply-lined face chalk-white. Hardy approached the group silently and whispered to Burke, the nearest man.

"Where's the chief surgeon? Where's Mr Beatty?"

"Amputating, sir," Burke answered. "Midshipman's leg. Back here in a moment."

The exchange had roused the Admiral. Hardy went and knelt beside him, reaching out to grasp the thin left hand in his big fist for a moment. It was icy cold.

"Hardy!" Nelson's high voice was clear, but speech was evidently a painful effort. "You've come at last. How goes the battle?"

"Very well, my lord. We've taken twelve, maybe fourteen, of the enemy. It's not over, though, and I can't stay below for long."

"I hope none of ours have struck, Hardy?"

"No, my lord—never fear it." The flag-captain's deep voice

was as reassuring as he could make it. "But five of their van have tacked to bear down on *Victory* and I must be on deck when we engage."

"Have you signalled for assistance?"

"Yes, my lord—to *Spartiate* and *Minotaur*. I don't doubt we'll give them a drubbing between us."

Nelson was silent for a few seconds, and his next words were spoken in a low voice. "I'm a dead man, Hardy—I'm going fast. It will all over with me soon. Come nearer. Nearer."

Hardy bent forward until his ear was close to the Admiral's lips. The words were just audible above the distant irregular boom of cannon.

"Let dear Lady Hamilton have my hair, and all other things belonging to me."

Before Hardy could respond the chief surgeon arrived, hastily scrubbing his hands and arms with a reddened cloth. He nodded satisfaction as he saw the flag-captain.

"Glad you're here, sir," he said. "The Admiral's asked for you more than once. How is he?"

"He seems pretty comfortable." Hardy tried to keep the anxiety out of his tone. "That's a good sign, sure. A sign he's going to be on his feet before long, Mr Beatty—eh?"

Nelson's voice answered. "Oh no, Hardy. That's impossible—my back's shot through. Beatty will tell you that."

Hardy looked a question at the surgeon. Beatty nodded and turned away. Swallowing an unprecedented lump in his throat, Hardy shook the Admiral's bony claw again and returned on deck.

Victory's starboard broadside fired as he came up into air and daylight. Quilliam, leaping a litter of fallen blocks and rigging which was in process of being cleared away, hurried across to him.

"Is it true the Admiral's killed, sir?" he demanded.

Hardy's narrowed gaze was on the cluster of ships vaguely seen through the drifting gunsmoke. Beyond the fact that the

Tricoleur fluttered from three of the mastheads in sight he could make out little.

"Report to me, Mr Quilliam, if you please," he said sharply. "*Spartiate* and *Minotaur*—did they acknowledge?"

Victory's guns thundered again. An answering broadside screamed overhead and a section of the poop rail vanished in a rain of fragments. The first lieutenant replied as soon as he could be heard.

"*Spartiate*'s coming up on our starboard bow, sir, and *Minotaur*'s right on the beam. She's engaging now." He hesitated. "And—and Nelson, sir?"

Hardy glared at him. Then his irritation gave place to an odd sort of pride. The passing of Nelson would mean more to a good many Englishmen than victory or defeat.

"The Admiral's badly hurt," he said shortly. "I'll thank you to go for'ard, Mr Quilliam, and see that every gun on the larboard side is double-shot loaded."

To larboard of the flagship there was no immediate danger. The long sullen swell there supported the ruin of the *Redoutable* a cable-length away and beyond her a group of captured French ships; floating spars with men clinging to them rose and fell on the discoloured waters and boats pulled busily to and fro picking up survivors. But attack might yet come from that side. Hardy ran up to the poop to gaze to starboard, where a renewal of cannon-fire indicated that *Minotaur* had engaged one or other of the advancing French ships. One of the Frenchmen, a 74, could be seen through the smoke; it was she who had been firing at *Victory*. But now her brown flank with the two rows of gaping gunports was turning away, and he could see men aloft setting her royals. She was running for it. A roar of cheering from the deck below him and Quilliam's yell of "Cease fire!" were followed by a sharp double explosion some distance away to his left. Through the clearing wisps of smoke he saw *Spartiate* moving towards the fleeing Frenchman, firing her bow-chasers. It looked as if *Victory*'s part in the battle was over. He could go to the dying man in the orlop.

Except that Beatty, the surgeon, now knelt at Nelson's left side, the scene in the lamplit gloom was unchanged. Hardy knelt on his other side and they grasped hands.

"My lord," Hardy said, forcing himself to smile, "I've come to congratulate you on a complete victory."

Nelson, who had not relinquished his hold on Hardy's hand, nodded feebly. "How many have we taken?"

"It's not yet possible to say, my lord, but I'll answer for fourteen or fifteen."

"That's well—but I'd bargained for twenty." The high voice, very weak now, strengthened suddenly. "Now anchor, Hardy—anchor."

"My lord, I—um—I suppose Admiral Collingwood will take over—"

"Not while I live, I hope! No—do *you* anchor, Hardy."

The Admiral had spoken with an access of energy that now seemed to have exhausted him. Hardy had to bend forward to catch the next whispered utterance.

"Don't throw me overboard, Hardy."

"Of course not—of course not."

"You know what to do. And take care of my dear Lady Hamilton—take care of poor Lady Hamilton." His voice faded to a thin whisper. "Kiss me, Hardy."

The flag-captain touched the pallid cheek with his lips. Nelson drew his hand from Hardy's grasp.

"Now I am satisfied. Thank God, I've done my duty."

Hardy rose slowly to his feet and stood looking down at him: this small skinny man, one-armed, one-eyed, a bundle of odd contradictions. Vain and yet valorous, weak and yet unearthly strong, he had today set his country free from the double threat of invasion and blockade, had won against odds the greatest naval victory in British history. He was everything that Hardy was not, and yet the big man standing bowed beneath the low deckhead felt that a part of himself lay there dying, that the blazing spirit soon to be snuffed out like a candle had lit an answering flame in his own breast. And that bright flame in Nelson—he knew it in a sudden flash of revelation—had had to be fed by love, by affection. Without that constant fuel it could not have burned. It was the reason for Nelson's desire for adulation; it was the reason for Emma Hamilton. It was the reason for his strange request that his friend and flag-captain should kiss him. That symbol and assurance of affection had given him the courage he needed to face the ending of life and all that it held for him. On an irresistible impulse, Hardy dropped to his knees and kissed the Admiral's forehead. The drooping eyelids quivered. The high voice was very faint.

"Who is that?"

"It's Hardy."

"God bless you, Hardy," said Nelson feebly.

Hardy got blindly to his feet and stumbled away; he was not going to make a fool of himself in front of those others. He came on deck and stood for a moment to let the slight breeze cool his face. The last gunfire had died away to silence. Across the leeward horizon lay a bank of lavender fog formed by powder-smoke, and against this background a score of great ships, near and far, lay in the golden light of the westering sun. They were ships of the aftermath, spent, battered, their sails torn and riddled and their flags scarcely stirring on the evening air. There was a solemn beauty in the scene; through its glowing colour shone the glory and the tragedy of human life, the perpetuity of man's greatness and the finality of his end. Hardy, uplifted beyond himself for a space, felt a surge of emotion almost too strong to be borne.

Then it was gone, instantaneously as darkness follows light when a lamp is blown out. He saw with other eyes now. One of the larboard jeer-bitts had been shot away and would have to be replaced; so would the missing section of the poop rail. That mizen topmast hanging aloft must be lowered without delay and a jury topmast rigged. He was Captain Hardy of the *Victory* again; plain Tom Hardy, stolid, careful, uninspired as he would always be. Here came Quilliam, and with him Bunce the carpenter and half-a-dozen others, each with his report and his problem. He had taken a step to meet them when a hand was laid on his arm and he turned.

It was Doctor Scott, the chaplain. His bony face was wet with tears and he spoke his message with difficulty.

"Sir—the end has come. Lord Nelson is dead."

EPILOGUE

Outside the church the icy fog of December hung on the Nova Scotian shores and hid the squadron in Halifax harbour. Inside was light and colour, gold and blue and white; wedding gowns and naval uniforms, a joyful noise of organ and choir for the marriage ceremony between Captain Sir Thomas Hardy, Baronet, and Anne Louisa Emily, daughter of Admiral Sir George Berkeley commanding on the North American station.

A handsome couple, whispered the ladies of Halifax in the congregation, but well for her that he's so large a man—she being such a buxom lass herself, and tall with it. And indeed Captain Hardy, bending his head to kiss his new-made wife, had not so very far to bend. There was a moment, before that sealing of a contract, when the great church with its lights and music vanished from Hardy's sight and he was back in *Victory*'s orlop two years ago, stooping to kiss the thin cold cheek of a dying hero. The vision passed instantly. The cheek so close to his mouth was round and rosy. But Anne turned with a smile and a blush and gave him her lips.